The Wounded Reindeer

Sadete Halilaj

To my husband for his unwavering faith and confidence in me.

First published in USA in 2015 by Lulu

Copyright © S. Halilaj 2015

The right of Sadete Halilaj to be identified as the author of this Work has been asserted by her in accordance with the Copyright, Design and Patents Act 1998.

All rights reserved.

No parts of this publication may be reproduced, stored in retrieval, or transmitted in any form or by any means, without the prior permission in writing of the publisher, nor be otherwise circulated in any form of binding or cover other than that in which it is published and without a similar condition including this condition being imposed on the subsequent purchaser.

ISBN 978-1-326-29035-1

"If you can force your heart and nerve and sinew

To serve your turn long after they are gone,

And so hold on when there is nothing in you

Except the Will which says to them: Hold on!"

Rudyard Kipling

It was spring and a light, warm breeze, blowing from the west, stroked the frail new leaves on the tree branches. The birds with their elated chirps seemed to thoroughly enjoy the light breeze. It came as a soft humming tune on earth's spring invigorated lips. The farmers, at this time of year, had to keep themselves assiduous to the land. They had to love and work it with devotion if they were to look forward to a plentiful harvest. The land was passed down by their ancestors.

It was the land that had been turned into battlefields many times over the centuries. It had quenched its simmering summery thirst with hot blood from the veins of her sons. Many times over it was sown with bones and skulls. The land was sacred to them and the seeds had to be sown with love and tenderness. They felt in their hearts the dead ancestors standing and watching that the land was tended to with love. And when they worked *the land*, the farmers converted themselves into 'lahutas'* whose strings would turn the murmur of the long working hours into blissful music.

They loved *the land*.

Although the farmers had not been able to closely follow the changing political climate, the building tension and trepidation could easily be read on their anxious face expressions. Externally, these spring days were tranquil for all the farmers in the village. But an air of expectancy, resembling a dark cloud impregnated with heavy rain and ready to strike thunder, hung all around.

Vera was absorbed in her grandfather's story. It was 'The bramble and the grape vine,' her favourite story. This time, strangely, he was reading it to her. *'A small bramble was living in a narrow hedgerow,'* granddad's voice echoed into her ears. *"When, the rain omitted its obligation during the summer droughts, its eyes turned green with envy for a small grape vine. The grape had its roots in a small spring stream. Its liveliness and good health were transparent, for anyone to see, on its beaming green leaves. The bramble would look sadly at its withering leaves. If the rain took longer in landing on earth, they would turn brown and die way. The bramble kept comparing its leaves with the grapes'.*

One day the bramble had a sneaky idea. 'Oh, hello lively grape', said the bramble chirpily. 'Hello' the grape answered cautiously as he sensed the ghost of brambles' dark thoughts flickering around.

'What can I do for you little bramble? asked the grape intermittently ignoring the ghost.

'I would be really obliged if you made some room for my branches. I am getting very thirsty up here, and a very little space would save my life' the bramble uttered its plea.

'And we can be very good friends as I can lend you a hand should you need it' the bramble added quickly, manipulating its way in.

'O....kay' the grape agreed reluctantly.

The grape knew that it was doing very well on its own and did not need any help. But its generous and hospitable nature did not allow it to turn the bramble way. 'If God has granted him permission to drink from the deep well of life, than I can spare a few cups from my stream' thought the grape. He moved a little to make space for the bramble. Very soon the bramble wrapped the grape vines in its prickly thorn branches. Gradually, it acquired all the space and the grape was throttled.

'What are you doing bramble?' the grape requested. 'You're suffocating me' he added surprised and shocked by bramble's behaviour. 'If living under my lively branches does not fit to your liking you can leave mister grape,' the bramble pointed to the road arrogantly. 'But……..but' the grape mumbled. 'No buts, just leave' the bramble interrupted cynically, brooking no arguments. Then the poor grape thought of leaving, but where to? That was its own home, it always had been. Had the sanctuary given to the bramble, signed its own end? And the grape, ever since has spent hundreds of years fighting for its own existence. And cursing itself for giving that sanctuary in the first place.

Vera, Vera!
 Someone was interrupting the story in her dream.
She had missed her granddad and his stories. Vera was enjoying this short retrieve of her childhood. '
'Vera, get up!'
Someone shook her from her sleep. In her efforts to wake up, Vera could not indicate the person behind the voice. *Was it auntie Mira?* Vera had been living with her and her six family members for the past four years.
'Vera, Vera!'
The voice grew stronger and more determinant. This time the sleep loosened its grip, but her grandfather's voice was still

echoing in her ears, *'fight.........ting for ......its o........wn existenceeeeeeee'.*

'Oh for goodness sake child, get up!'
Vera realised the urgency in her mother's voice.
'What is it mum?' she asked while her brain was trying to grasp the reality around.

She was in her parent's home, in the village. She'd sought for a quiet place to study, prior to her coming up exams.
It was her final year in the professional school for nurses. But her dream was to become a doctor. And that more than anything had been the driving force behind her persistence to do well and land a place at the university.
First, she had not even liked the idea of going way from the city and all her friends who'd get together and go out from time to time.
She'd miss going to the cinema, or walking by the riverbank under the warm spring afternoons. Above all she'd enjoy the company of ....., oh no, she wouldn't dare to even mention his name in her most inner thoughts, let alone revealing to her mother loving him.

She could not describe the feeling derived from a wonderful light that had entered her. It had lit up all the deepest corners of her heart.
Vera could not describe the afternoons when they, her and Milo, would look deep in each- others' eyes getting hazy in the divine love.
And the world around them would stand still.
They did not speak much.

They just walked hand in hand on the quiet river bank, many sunny afternoons. They'd feel the tremor of their hands. The tremor transmitted their love like the murmur from the rivulets of a small stream joining the sea. Love had extended its fiery fingers and had clutched their hearts tightly.

Vera felt that she was not ready to tell her mother.

Not just yet, not until all the exams were over. Then, and only then, she'd stumble on a path into launching a conversation, which would lead to revealing the 'love of her life'. There had been many a time when she'd found herself rehearse the tête-à-tête.

'Mum, I know a very *handsome* man', she'd emphasise handsome, hinting what would follow, whom I am in love with' dragging down her gaze, which would miss match the tone of her voice.

The eyes, Vera could not help, even when rehearsing, but lower them down. She was aware that some time ago she'd promised her mother to put on hold the romance side of her life until at a later stage of her university studies.

Once in her mother's warm embrace she'd become oblivious to all her misgivings about coming to the quiet country life. And she had the news that was nesting in her chest, like a caged eagle longing to ascend in the vast expanse of the blue sky. She'd elected coming to the country, as her two little twin cousins, with their in turns crying and screaming at each other, had made sure that there was not a single quiet spot in the house where Vera could escape to.

'What's the matter mum?' Vera asked again, standing on the bed, rubbing her eyes, puzzle, and initial notes of fear merging in her voice.

Being asked to get up by 3am, and urgently as it appeared, did not sound as if a normal event was about to commence. She looked up on her mother's face. The dim light released by the small bedside lamp, did not help in reading it. Vera sprang on her feet and went for the light switch.

'No!' her mothers' firm voice and grasp on both hands, rooted her on the spot.

What could possibly be so wrong that made her ever calm mother act like that?

Vera was trying to reason in anticipating the situation.

'Listen carefully', her mother loosened the grip on Vera's hands while placing them on Vera's shoulders. She pushed her lightly to sit back on the bed.

Vera felt the warmth of the bed covers crumpled underneath her and waited for her mother to speak again.

'The whole village is up. The Serbs are raiding and from what I've heard tonight they are………, she paused inhaling deeply… -killing,' she uttered allowing a long sigh out with her last word. Zana would not have wanted her children alarmed.

For her Vera was still a child although at nineteen.

But the time was ticking away very fast. There was no time for pussyfooting around. The danger was present and the risks too great.

'You must take your brother and run to your father's safe place,' Zana continued in the same anxious, filled with fear for their lives, tone.

She was incognizant of Vera's trembling shoulders.

'You're not to come out, until I come and tell you that it is safe to,' Zana whispered to her daughter, while adding to herself *'if I'm alive.'*

'Stay put and do not move for whatever reason' alarm and panic blatant in her voice, words almost tumbling over one another.

Vera sat there completely mute.

Her mother was issuing out such unusual orders.

She needed a considerable amount of time to elapse before the information of such orders was fully digested by her brain, considering the state of it, only a few minutes after a deep serene sleep.

Labouring to hastily grapple it all, her eyes widened.

Did her mother mean that if found in the house, their own home, they'd be killed?

Why?

What had she done?

What had her young brother done? He was only seven.

Could they be killing children?

This last question struck a chord within her.

She'd heard far too many old stories about Serb soldiers and how they never spared even children as young as still in their mother's belly.

Her grandfather's voice echoed in her ears '*They'd cut open the pregnant woman's body and get the foetus out using their swords.*'

'If not for yourself think about your brother' her mother's pleading voice interrupted her granddad's echoing voice.

His voice seemed to be in her head since she woke up.

'He needs you,' Zana turned her back on her, grabbed a bag which she found at the foot of the bed. She swiftly thrust some of Vera's clothes in it.

'He needs you,'

Zana was aware of her daughters' obstinate selflessness nature. She reiterated the last sentence as if comprehending her daughters' wordless reluctance to leave their mother behind. Vera said nothing feeling the panic distend inside her.

She stood up.

Her mother was motioning for her to follow.

She felt slightly unsteady.

Her grandfather's voice resumed echoing.

What on earth was happening?

She was in a trance like state.

'*I hope you'll never witness their atrocities my pet, but I doubt it.*'

He'd said it so many times after telling her bedtime stories.

One of most horror ones had been her great grandfather's story. He'd been a young child when Serbian soldiers had killed all his family. Made obtuse by the tremendous fear witnessing his family being savagely killed and his mother's body fallen onto him after beheaded, had saved him his life.

It seemed as if he was spared to describe the barbarisms that Serbs had attacked the Albanian population at the time.
The bloodshed experienced that day had carved itself in his brain. Until he'd died, aged 83, he'd describe in detail his family's encounter with its death inflicted by the swords of Serbian 'nationalists', as they had called themselves.
Time had not managed to alter or eradicate from his memory any of the moments of that fateful day. His four brothers and sisters along with both their parents and an uncle that happened to be there, seven people, were butchered in a few minutes.

'But, now it should be different for God's sake,' Vera's brain started working at last.

It cannot be true that the old devils, from ancient times, are throwing away the grave stones and emulate the old stories once again!?
'Aren't we supposed to be civilised and solve our problems with talks, without the need of *swords*, I mean guns?' -she asked herself. Although she unable to pinpoint at any real problem that would cause the two nations to fight for.
'Vera! Vera!' Her mothers' anxious voice interrupted her rational thoughts.
'Hurry up, there is not much time' Zana was at the edge of shouting at her daughters sluggish movements.
At any other time Zana would stomach it, but not tonight.
'You may have to run away for some time, so better get some of your clothes in here and quick!' command, love and ambiguity for what would happen, assorted in her voice.

She managed to find two pairs of Vera's jeans and a cropped top, the one, Vera observed, she wore for Milo in their last afternoon walk.
Zana was shoving them in the bag.
It was so unlike her mother.
She used to hate the least flaws in clothes.
Zana went at the small chest, in the corner, and opening the first drawer she asked 'Where do you keep your underwear? I always had them folded in here.'
'Here, here they are' Vera hastily answered digging them out of a carton box.
She'd needed the drawers for the pile of books she'd brought from the city. Otherwise it would have been all over the floor. She kept her room clean and tidy. It was her pride. But then her mother had taught her really well.
Vera handed to Zana, a bunch of neatly folded knickers and a few other underwear items. Her mother snatched them and thrust them in the bag too.
'Look after your brother, he needs you,' the digestion of these words in her brain, brought a halt to her breathing.
Her heart trembled in her chest like a wounded reindeer cornered by its hungry predator.
Did it mean that her mother might be killed?
Chocked for breath, Vera felt panic engulfing her. Her legs went limp...
'This may be the last time that my mother spoke to me,' this thought, dark as a moonless night, lodged itself deeply in her brain.

'We cannot leave without you, mum,' deep begging tones in her statement.

She too was fully aware of her mothers' stubborn selflessness when it came to her children.

'We can't leave you behind,' Vera tried again following her mother in her brother's bedroom.

Zana said nothing.

She got up her son, who luckily did not object at being awoken up that early.

'He's still asleep for all I know' Zana thought slipping a warm hand knitted jumper on top of his nightclothes.

Although the spring had started perching in with sunny and quite warm days, the nights were still very chilli. Zana slung the bag on her back.

Pulling Vera with her left hand and Joni with her right, started towards the rear of the house.

Once the back door was open for them to pass in the garden, they heard the mayhem nearing their house.

Cries for help and agonising screams that only flesh being ripped off could muster, were piercing the night air.

She heard glass being smashed and household wares being kicked, sporadic gunshots and at times a distinguished angry voice in Serbian prevailed, barking orders.

'The ancient devils are back after all' Vera thought horror-struck.

The thought of leaving her mother behind in this situation, triggered a wave of hot tears.

Every second counted now.
They both, mother and daughter were aware of it.
Zana passed the bag in Vera's left hand. In her right hand she gently placed Jon's warm hand.
Parting with her children's hands sent a piercing chill through her heart.
'Would she see them again?'
She had to be harsh, perhaps for the first time in her life, and push them through the door.
'Now run' she whispered in case of being heard behind the wooden fence.
She pushed them, gently, but determinately out and closed the gate slowly.
She stood there waiting for them to run, as if making sure that they would be out of danger.
Vera could not bring herself to moving away. The reason behind her mother's stay was palpable.
She was throwing her life in grave danger to shield that of her children.
Vera could not command her legs to move.
Swinging the gate back open and dragging her brother

along, threw herself in her mothers' open arms.

For a moment there was silence between the three of them. They laboured hard holding back their tears, in a warm and very dear embrace.

Vera and Joni had their heads resting on their mother's chest. Vera could feel her mother's palpitating heartbeats, and felt her throat ache, as she tightened it further to hold her rapidly welling hot tears.

Zana wrapped her arms around both her babies as they clung tightly onto her.

'You must go now,' Zana was trying hard to hold it together. Her desperate tone deceived her.

The moon reflected a faint light as if showing them the path that had to be followed. It was the last glimpse of light, before the moon retired for the night. The earth soon would plunge into pitch darkness. Just before dawn.

They released each other slowly and started in opposite directions.

Vera and Joni started towards hope for their lives. While, Zana trotted back in, towards uncertainty and death perhaps.

That night death seemed to be lurking around like hungry vultures hovering over decaying carcasses.

With their mother out of sight they started, instinctively, running towards the hiding place.

There were high pitch shrieks, shouting and loud cries that chilled Vera's heart. A cacophony of human cries, hard banging doors which seemed to be flung off the hinges and a dog's mad barking, resembling the voices of militia commandants issuing orders, sounded very near.

Vera had knowledge of the existence of this place, only a few days back. From all she'd heard from neighbouring villages, her mother, had anticipated a possible raid from VJ*. Their house one would be one of the first to be raided, as it was Besim Gashi's home.

She had taken Vera to the place.

On their way there, they had been very cautious of prying eyes. Her mother had told her when it was build.

'*Dug*' suits it better Vera had thought silently once inside. However, her mother had never disclosed the real reason for visiting the place.

Vera had thought herself mature enough in her mother's eyes as the real reason for this family secret being unveiled to her.

The memory of the times when she'd missed her father, and now discovered that he'd been so near and yet so far, made her, for a moment, feel resentful towards her parents.

It occurred to her that her parents had not trusted her with this secret.

Apparently they had considered her a child and only a single word slipped from her to any of her childhood friends would have dragged her father into a grave situation.

But, would I have uttered a single word to anyone?

No, of course not' she reassured herself.

Though deep down she felt, she'd given Lena, her best childhood friend, a small, tiny clue about the place.

She would have felt more mature with the secret and in efforts to make it visible in her friends' eyes; she'd throw some hints to let Lena know that she was carrying a big secret.

But, where is my father now?

Her thoughts resembled her panicky running bare feet down the ravine, towards the safe place.

Is it really safe?

These questions set her brain spinning.

Where on earth was he, when needed most?

Although deep down she suspected if anyone was able to do much.

'*Look after yourself*' she'd heard him say to Zana whilst adjusting his backpack one night.

During that day Vera had 'sniffed', some peculiarity in her parents' behaviour.

Her mother had appeared very emotional. Although trying hard to conceal it by saying, 'I'm not feeling well,' could not fool Vera for she never remembered her mother complaining, even when trembling from fever and high temperature.

The way they, both her parents, seemed to avoid one another's eyes, had been the first clue of something going on.

It seemed as if they were in pain. A small gaze at each other's eyes would surface the ache they were keeping under a firm lid. Vera had told herself she'd better stay 'on lookout' that night.

'Look out' was Lena's and her code when they were dubious of their friends, siblings and even their parents' movements. Whenever convinced something was being kept from them, 'look out' was their secret code into the discovery of the mystery. They would communicate it to each other even without saying it loud.

A pair of big eyes, fretfully, looking in opposite directions, drawn on a piece of paper, meant; 'Something fishy is going on, better inspect for ourselves.'

But, often, when it involved adults, it meant the bedroom door ajar, forgotten of course, and forcing yourself awake. The last bit was quite difficult when they were young, but had become easier growing older.

That night the 'look out' had paid off.

'Take great care of Vera and Joni,' had said her father. Concern and trepidation for his dearests' safety while absent, evident in his deep voice.

And *'I know you will, you always have'* he'd added kissing Zana warmly.

'He'd come and kiss my brother and I goodbye' Vera had surmised.

Better play fast asleep.

But as her father had neared her bed she could not help herself but break the pretence of fast asleep.

She'd extended her arms to reach for a warm hug.

Her move had sprung a look of surprise to quickly be replaced with a pleasant one on her father's handsome face.

'You look after your brother' he'd said while pulling her in his embrace and kissing her smooth fair hair on top of her head.

'I know you will,' he'd added reassuring her of his trust, while bending over his then three years old son, kissing him goodbye.

It had been the last that she'd seen of him.

'*Take care of your brother*' her father and mother had said. They had said it in different times, different contexts, and meant different protections.

Her father had asked her to look after him in a way that he would not scratch and graze his knees and arms when playing around.

While, her mother had asked her to protect him from being killed.

However, they both had placed their trust on her.

'And I will, take care of him' she thought almost audibly, tightening her hand's grip on that of her brother's.

It struck her that her brother's silent walk, very unusual for him, had made her oblivious of his presence.

Strange, because she'd been pulling him by his hand, since they parted with their mother.

She thought of talking to him, and then decided against the idea, fearing being heard on the other side of the path, which was camouflaged by thick dense bramble bushes.

It seemed as this spring they'd been left, deliberately, to grow out of control.

No one had cared to prune them, or did not want to.

It became obvious to her, that though nobody had talked overtly, people all around her, spare herself, knew or were at least expecting that something was about to transpire.

'I've been too caught up in myself and my love to have noticed anything' she thought bitterly.

People, unlike her, had tried to prepare themselves for the worst. Though nobody would really be able to contemplate how far Serbs would go this time.//
A huge bomb blast axed her thoughts as it forced the ground into a tremendous shiver.//
She had to steady herself and her brother from falling.//
 Vera could not locate the exact place.//
However, it must have been near; she'd heard and felt the air quiver just before the blast.//
The earth had shaken in waves, nanoseconds before the blast invaded the dawn air and deafened Vera.//
 Everything around lit up for a few seconds.//
For a slight moment, after the blast, it all went silent.//
Then a fresh wave of cries, shouts curses and shotguns rose.//
The moonlight had faded completely by then and the earth had plunged in pitch darkness.//
 She had to feel her way through the path.//
She kept her free hand in front of her face so the thorny thick branches whacked her hand in her face's stead.//
 She'd hear the swift noise emitted by her backpack in contact with the branches after their first encounter with her hand. Her senses had been dulled.//
She wasn't feeling the sting and slashes that the prickly thorns were opening on her hand's skin.//
There was blood trickling down her little finger, yet she could feel nothing more than the stickiness of the blood on her palm.//
The fear of what might happen to their mother and//
themselves had outstripped the physical pain.//

The path led to a small stream.
It was used to fill the small dam build in the centre of their fertile land.
During the summer it'd be used to water the crop fields all around it.
Vera's uncle, Fatmir Shala, Zana's brother, had contributed in buying and installing a new water system.
It had made the last couple of years, by far, easier for Zana.
Since her father's in law passing away, she'd been single handed in maintaining the farm. Even two-three years before his death, he'd become so fragile with age that his involvement in the farm had caused more distractions then help.
His son, Besim, had never totally linked himself with the inherited land. He'd had no intentions in becoming what his father would have liked and wanted, a good farmer.
He'd become a university lecturer instead.
Later he'd left university for journalism. It seemed as university halls had been too confined for him and his ideas.
With journalism he'd expanded his audience. But soon he'd found himself in trouble with Serbian authorities, and not long after that, in prison.
Zana had been brought up in a farm, and although her father had paid for her education and had wanted her to be a doctor, she'd resigned to maintaining her husband's farm.
For the first few months of her marriage, Zana had been faced with her father's in-law cold look and dismissive manner.
She'd sensed the reason behind, and being prudent as she was, had just gone along with it. She'd foreseen she'd bring him

around in due course. Even so, deep down it had bothered her, and she'd tried her very best to get entry in her father's in law good books.

He had revealed later contritely 'My son had gone for the looks.'

It had dominated his thoughts since their first meeting with her after the engagement. He'd regretted not having enjoyed his son's wedding.

The bride had been blissful, as if coming out of a fairy tale.

To her father in law, her pale face; with large brown eyes and the warm rainbow light emanated from them, weren't features of a farmer's wife. Her delicate long fingered hands had been the first hint in making him think, 'this is not the daughter in law I wanted.' Her slender young body looked prone to being blown miles away by the first autumn winds that grazed all the fields in their path.

Zana had loved and respected him, however. She'd pretended as if she'd never caught him casting askew glances. Despite him being hostile towards her, she'd followed him in his daily chores around the farm.

Very soon he'd discovered that, hard work, brain, and beauty were accurately balanced in his daughter in law.

Her beautiful and taciturn at the same time face features, had earned her his respect.

For he knew from first-hand experience that talk was the last needed in a farm.

She'd not even asked if she should do the chores around.

She'd watched him closely and carefully the way he carried out certain tasks and then gone on in doing them, trying really hard in maintaining his way.

Over the years he'd started to trust her managing the farm and admitted at not wishing for a better daughter in law.

She'd reinstated the farmer son he'd always wanted.

If he'd had two or three sons, at least one would have cared for the farm. But his wife had died giving birth to his daughter, Mira, his second child, when Besimi had been five.

He'd never remarried.

His mother had helped him bring up the two children.

Vera was wondering how long, the ravine path was. That night it seemed exceedingly long.

When she felt her feet immerse into water, she knew they weren't far. And some sense of relief sipped through her like water in thirsty earth.

She reminded herself to carry her brother, so his feet would be kept dry and warm. While holding him, she checked if he had his shoes on.

She found, like her, he hadn't.

Hastening as they were it had not even occurred to her or her mother to look for their shoes.

'Pointless to carry him then,' she told herself.

She carried him nevertheless.

Once on the other side of the stream, she kept on the right and started feeling with her hand for the small wooden door.

If it can be called a door, 'a box lid more like' Vera had thought when her mother had instructed her how to open and shut it from inside.

She'd seen its position.

It was underneath a large oak tree surrounded by thick bramble bushes protruding from the earth.

And she found it.

As she took hold of the handle and was about to lift it up, she stood for a moment listening to the nearing chaos that had reigned since her mother had woken her up.

The piercing screams raised, in short intervals and from different directions, conveyed unimaginable horrors befalling the source of these sounds.

She lifted up the small entry door and put it aside slowly, maintaining an easy way in replacing it back in its former position once they were in the 'box'.

'Here we are Joni' she whispered feeling their way through the hole, gently pulling her brother.

They both had to kneel down and walk in all fours through a short narrow tunnel.

She assumed that they'd arrived as she was feeling with her hands the straw bed she'd seen when she'd come with her mother.

The straw released swishing noises while they sat on it.

They sat close together, keeping warm and reassuring each other with their presence.

Vera sat there staring in total darkness, and just then noticing the sharp, pungent of wet earth scent trouncing in her nostrils.

After a while she could listen to her brother's rhythmic breathing.

She thought him asleep.

Slowly, as not to wake him, she placed the backpack underneath him, and took his head onto her lap.

'We can't afford to be ill at this very dangerous situation' she thought bitterly.

Why did they have to leave their warm beds in the first place? Why isn't our father protecting us?

Her thoughts back at her fathers' whereabouts.

He'd become a journalist, she assumed, to make more room for himself and his deprecations.

But how good had he been as a journalist?

An awful lot good! Vera told herself.

Otherwise he would not have found himself in trouble with the, *mainly* Serb, local authorities.

She thought, *mainly*, because the new presidents' arrival had seen, to most Albanians that held some position in the governing, their sacking.

If resisted being fired, some fake faults 'were brought to light', and if the resistance had been severe, their faults had become severer, and they'd ended up in prison.

However the Serbs had kept some puppets with a dual use. First, they were used as tokens, suggesting that a mixed body, which matched its population, governed Kosovo.

Second, keeping on those who obeyed, the authorities conveyed the message of fear and obedience to the masses.

All those that tuned out of the Serbian governmental farce, pissed them off.

And they would take drastic measures to punish those who managed tuning out.

Vera checked upon her brother again.

He'd not uttered a single word since that abrupt wake up.

She stroked his face lightly to see if he had his eyes closed and slowly whispered;

'Listen, you stay here and please do not move, I'll go and see what's going on and I'll be back in a tick, okay!'

He did not make any move or release any sound, except for the rhythmical breathing.

She was not sure if he'd heard her and was reluctant to leave him in such a dark place, alone.

But the great fear for her mother's life won over the reluctance and she thought that her brother would be alright. That's what she told herself, anyhow.

What would be the time now?

Is it almost morning?

She removed, very slowly, the 'lid' door, and cocked her head outside.

Looked around, but nothing was clear enough to see.

The big grown bramble bushes looked larger now.

The first faint dawn light had come up from behind, casting big shadows in front of them.

As she was about to climb out, a huge bang, resembling a gunshot punctured the dawn air.

It caused her disregard the frightening shadows in front of her, and sprint towards the house.

She thought that the bang had come from their house.

She kept running unacquainted of her bare feet being hurt in contact with the sharp edged stones, and getting tangled in twigs and cut off branches from the bramble bushes.

She'd chosen the other side of the narrow path, behind the bushes.

There was a wider path and the bushes, were pruned fashionably, in a nice curved pattern. It seemed an unfinished task as the nippy bramble thorns appeared to easily find their way in Vera's feet.

The twigs and branches had been left lying around, across the path.

Some of them would stick on her pyjamas and she cursed herself for making the wrong choice in following this path as quicker, while trying to get them off.

It slowed her down.

Although the path she'd chosen led to her front door, she wouldn't dare approach from the front.

About fifteen metres before arriving at her home front door, she averted direction.

While jumping the garden fence, she felt that her left nightgown sleeve got caught on one of the pointing fence sticks.

It forced her to fall face flat on the grass.

Thank God the fence wasn't too high and she did not think that she'd hurt herself.

'Would I be feeling anything anyway' she thought as she approached the house from the back. While she'd been on the other side of the fence, she had heard a faint noise coming from her house. The noise coming from the cluster of houses just beneath theirs had overwhelmed it.
But once in the garden the noise was clear and strong.
She could depict on her mind which pan or table was being kicked, by the noise discharged in the air.
She could even hear their voices.
She could not fathom what was being said, however 'fucking bitch' in both languages shot heavily through her ear membrane. It was her mother at the receiving end of this abusive name calling, she reckoned.
Despite the slowly morning light settling around, the living room, which looked through a big window into the garden, was brightly lit.
Yet, from that position she could see nothing.
The window was too high.
Ignoring the fact that she could blow her cover, Vera decided to climb up the cherry tree and afford a better view.
Her feet were slippery with mud and blood from the torn skin from the bramble thorns, and she couldn't climb as easily as she'd thought.
She'd climbed it since she'd been six or seven and the tree trunk had been slimmer. The tree had grown larger and bigger. But then so had she, taller and stronger she'd become.
They had been in a silent competition.

Every spring when the cherries became ripe, she'd try climbing and she'd succeed.

So, she must not fail now.

She lifted her right foot and wiped the mud clean from its sole on her left leg pyjamas.

Then she did the same with her left foot, wiping its sole on the right leg pyjamas.

'That's better, now I can climb you' she directed the tree trunk in the same way as she had when she'd been younger.

She'd thought, back then, that the tree grew larger to defeat and prevent her from grabbing the succulent deep red cherries off its branches.

After three attempts she managed to cling onto it and slowly, with great efforts, climb up.

She had three years that she hadn't climbed the tree. She'd been way the last three springs, to enjoy defeating the old friend and eating ripe cherries straight off its branches.

However, her mother had sent down to the city, once in two or three days, during the ripeness season, a large basket.

She would cover it with a hand embroidered, pristine white and carefully pressed cotton cloth. All her little cousins would hover over it and would fill their little hands full of sweet ripe cherries. Then they'd run outside to share with their friends and continue playing.

Every time she'd eat from the wood woven basket, she would long being home and climbing the cherry tree.

She reached the branch where she knew, she'd been up there countless times, would have a complete view of the living room. As she was about to sit on one of the branches, she heard a cracking noise relished from their back doors' rusted hinges.
She jumped out of her skin.
The released judder at being caught off guard almost knocked her down backwards.
A last, very quick body instinct to save itself propelled her into lurching with both her hands towards a branch.
It stood inches above her head.
The move caused a considerable amount of branch quiver.
 She looked down and was mortified to find a Serbian paramilitary coming out.
He had on a faded shade of green uniform.
The jacket was patched with many pockets, in which knife handles and a small pistol's bottom could easily be noticed.
He had a small torch in his left hand.
There was no need for it as dawn had settled completely and every object in the garden was clear enough to see.
In his right hand he was holding a big gun, Kalashnikov type, ready for fire at the slightest possible move.
Despite the chill dawn, Vera felt beads of hot sweat forming on her forehead and her whole body succumbed into numbness. Her brain was made indolent by the sheer fear she was feeling. However, it still was able to warn her for the luck she had in having her hands latched in the branch over her head. Otherwise, she'd have plummeted right in front of him if it was for that last instinctive move.

And he, doubtlessly, would've had her shot at without her body reaching the ground.

She could clearly see his pointing finger cemented in the weapon's trigger.

She forced her eyes tightly shut in a frantic attempt to not be seen.

Vera heard the crunch released by his boots in contact with the gravel, -mothers' efforts to prevent them from having muddy shoes when walking in the garden- which covered the path.

He is out for a tour around, she surmised.

The crunch faded for a while and then she heard it from the other side, on her back.

From behind he could, easily, spot her.

Fat beads of sweat started trickling down her spine.

Her heart was jumping out of her chest.

But, she had no intentions of giving up, but lingering on, she would.

She had no choice.

Vera prayed to God that he wouldn't spot her.

Suddenly, she heard him stop, just about beneath her.

She tightened her mouth to prevent her teeth clattering from being heard, and waited for a shotgun.

With her heart racing in her mouth, her eyes tightly shut and her neck tautly stretched, she waited thinking that in seconds hot bullets would sieve her body.

Her hands, though getting numb by the minute, were still, with all the strength she could muster, latched onto the branch above her head.

After a very short while, although for Vera seemed a century, for all the fear she was feeling.

Seeing that nothing transpired, she decided to risk a glance down.

She opened first one eye, than the other one and very slowly turned her head to look down.

She spotted him standing, scanning the garden, not more than two – three feet away from the cherry tree trunk.

After ostensibly satisfied that nothing moveable was on the ground, he was about to turn his eyes up. But a piercing shriek, coming from the house, stabbed the wet early morning air. Immediately he stopped probing around and scurried into the house.

The howling shriek, resembling that of a trapped squealing pig, made her forget the great danger lingering upon her.

She turned to look what had transpired in the house.

One of the Serbian paramilitary had blood covering all the right side of his face.

He kept his hand upon his right ear, pressing it as if to stop the blood. At the same time he continued to howl pacing frantically across the room.

Vera had a full view on his face, when, during his frenzied pacing, he came near the window.

His insipid face, with virtually absent eyebrows, he had them pulled down into his eye sockets, a big nose and big crooked teeth, clearly seen during the beast release sound process, gave Vera a terrible feeling.

He had a killers face.

Another paramilitary was bonding her mother with a rope. Vera recognised it as found in their barn. The rope was used for the horses to pull the cart when they gathered the harvest.

It seemed that they had had a thorough search.

The paramilitary that had been searching the garden came into the scene as he arrived in the living room.

It seemed that he was asking explanations as to what had transpired during his absence that had produced the beastly growls.

Vera was unable to hear their exchanges as the distance and the shut windows would not permit it.

She saw the garden soldier thrust the gun's barrel onto her mother's chest.

Vera's' brain went in mute fashion once again.

Was she about to witness her mothers' execution?

Was history replicating itself once more upon her family tree? She closed her eyes tightly to push the view out and waited for the bang in the same horrifying; if not worse state that she'd waited the bang on herself a few minutes previously.

Again, it did not come, and some, very small, fragile rays of hope entered her trembling body.

As she opened her eyes, she saw a fourth soldier trespassing in their living room.

They all were trying to tie her mother down.

It seemed that they had changed their minds about killing her, at least for the time being.

Her mother's fierce resistance against being tied up forced them to put their heavy guns aside and lend a hand to the one that had come up with this idea in the first place.

The rays of hope did not remain in Vera for long.

She quickly realised that they were up to a slow death for her mother.

Just simply kill her would not be entertaining.

They wanted to enjoy themselves in the process.

Why not, they were playing God.

'Sadist, bastards' Vera closed her eyes and thought about relishing a great shout for help.

As if she had the strength.

'But who would come to our rescue?'

A mighty bang of a bomb blast disconcerted her thoughts.

The tree gave a huge shudder.

Vera almost fell.

A new wave of cries and shouts and a burning smell arose in its wake.

It sounded very near.

Vera resumed her thoughts.

Who could possibly help?

The ones, supposed to be the rescuers are in fact the inflictors of this suffering.

The whole village was under siege.

They'd restricted Zanas' arms and legs to prevent her from releasing kicks and slaps towards them.

It took the four bastard's wrath to plant her down.

Vera saw the part eared crook come all over her mother. She could not fathom if he was kissing or biting her.

In the intervals between his head movements, he would pull back as if to admire his handy work, Vera noticed blood streaking down her mother's chin.

At one moment he ceased biting her and said something.

Zana said nothing.

Vera saw a splat of spit mottled with blood fly from her mother's mouth and land straight in crooks face.

With one hand he hastily wiped his face while with the other, quickly recovered a small handgun from its sheath strapped on his uniform trouser belt.

He placed the mouth pistol on her mother's bloody lips.

One of the three, who until then had been kept entertained by crooks' actions, put a hand out and, swiftly, pushed the gun way.

The crook said something and approached again toward Zana. This time he was not stopped.

Sprays of blood rained in the air and over crook's uniform as his gun butt landed heavily on her mother's face.

Seconds after her head hung down and her body followed.

She fell face first on the floor.

Her fall, she had both arms and legs roped, resembled a branch devoid tree trunk.

Rolling her body with their feet, they oscillated her initial fall position.

They had her on her back.

Vera was not sure if her mother was unconscious or was faking it to shut out those insipid faces around her. They started removing the rope, freeing her legs.

Something inside Vera started screaming;

'Kick them, and kick them hard on their faces. Kick the pigs now that you have a chance.'

But she noticed that her mother did not move.

They widespread her limply legs and started, using hand knives, slashing off her skirt and underwear.

Hastening to have her naked they were not bothered that with bits of clothes, bits of bloody flesh were flying around too.

All over her, they resembled feral dogs devouring fresh food that unexpectedly had landed in their claws.

Once her half down body was naked they took in undoing their trouser belts in hurry.

Horrified and utterly disgusted, Vera postulated what was to follow.

In great efforts to disappear from that moment, somewhere, anywhere, in the future or in the past, she forced her eyes tightly shut.

It did not matter where or when as long as she would not be at this torment present.

She did not notice that she was biting her bottom lip very hard. Her teeth, deep in her full lips, drew blood.

Vera's hands, clasped into tight fists, with nails digging in flesh, drew blood too.

Yet, she could feel no physical pain.

Her brain was once more, since that abrupt wake, in an unbearable painful swirling whirl.

Hundreds of questions, like a swarm of wasps encircling an over ripped sugar plum, attacked her brain viciously.

'What should I do?

Should I jump on mum's side and help her fight these filthy pigs off?

How do I fight all them four, they're all heavily armed?

Will mum's pain and humiliation tenfold if they turn on me as well?'

She tried to find a way out of these indecisive moments.

'What should I do?'

Her thoughts began to muddle up.

Suddenly, in these moments of great despair, she felt dizzy, and then tired as in dire need of a wink of sleep.

A considerable amount of her emotionally depleted brain cells were suggesting that this was only a nightmare.

It would wear off once awake.

However, there in some small parts of her brain a small amount of brain cells were intact.

They were fighting to keep her correlated to the reality around her.

But soon it seemed that they had lost the battle to the emotionally depleted brain cells.

She felt a vague physical pain and everything, despite the morning light beaming in all its natural strength, plunged into darkness.

It was all too painful and disgusting to contemplate.

****

'No, not now Milo, can't you see I'm busy' notes of suppressed anger in his father's voice.

Milo stepped back in the corridor closing the door slowly, relenting to his fathers' dark moods.

 Lately, these dark moods seemed to escalate in tempests upon the closest people to him.

He'd gone there intending to engage himself in a conversation with his father.

Milo had planned the way, slowly and tactfully, revealing his love for Vera to his father.

He'd talked to his mother.

Although she'd made some efforts to come out of that reverie in which she seemed to wrap herself of late, the enthusiasm she'd shown had been pitiful.

Milo had spilled out everything that'd been in his heart for quite some time, however.

'Her name is Vera, it means summer in Albanian, -that's how she is, a beautiful summer flower' he'd added with enthusiasm. He'd remembered the lines he'd written for Vera in his diary one night: *'Her graceful walk resembles the soft falling of the snow undisturbed by the wind. Her eyes derive a magic light that sips through my body and rests in my heart. The smile that adorns her lips outshines the crown diamonds that embellish the head of a queen. Her gentle soul is like a fresh drop of dew from the eyes of parting night onto young leaves of a sapling. '*

But he would not say any of that to anyone.

That was to remain only his and Vera's.

He told his mum about his plans to get engaged and his intentions of marrying Vera.

That of course after she'd finished university.

He knew that his parents expected his wife to be well brought up and educated. Foremost, she had to be pretty and very organised to keep up to his mother's immaculate order and cleanliness around the house. He was sure that Vera would live up to those expectations. If there was something new, she'd shape up quickly. He'd be there for her with his wholehearted love.

All his thoughts about Vera came to an abrupt halt when he remembered that cold look in his fathers' eyes. Although, far younger when he'd seen that look before, its retrieve was very clear.

He'd been peeping through the key hole of his fathers' workroom when his father's face had come into full view.

The blatant, cold anger envisaged in his fathers' eyes had sent shivering arrows down his spine.

He knew, from first- hand experience, what was meant in that look.

Scurrying way from the door, he'd tried to think who could be at the receiving end of his father's seething anger.

'Poor them' he'd thought behind the satin curtains in his bedroom window. He'd been watching his fathers' 'friends' leaving the house under the evening dim light.

Surprisingly, from above, their faces had appeared all alike, with stony cold looks.

Milo had blinked to make sure he was not asleep and having a nightmare with robot like stony faces.

 Not long after that 'meeting' with his comrades, his father, during a family meal, had announced the news:

'We're moving to Pristina.'

Mother's involuntarily fork falling on the table had sharpened the edge of the formidable look on father's face.

She, quickly and quietly, had picked the fork and carried on as if nothing unusual was said or a sudden subject was brought on the dining table.

Milo, had not failed to notice, mother's slightly trembling hand, and sad eyes while trying to conceal the shock that this unexpected news had delivered to her.

His mother's way of reaction had frozen a question on Milo's lips *'Why are we moving father?'*

He never dared to voice it.

From that moment he'd felt resentment start to build up.

Why he and his mother had no say and no choice in anything but follow every order given by him?

 They hadn't dared to even question his decisions. The logic had told Milo that his father was not one of those who one could argue with.

 So he'd kept quiet.

Within three weeks they had left their home and arrived, after a long drive in his father's 'Golf' late in evening, at the door of the new house.

It was all newly decorated and furnished but to Milo it had emanated a sense of loneliness. The thought of not seeing his friends again and leaving his caring grandparent behind, had plagued his heart.

The days when he went fishing down into the small river which gurgled its way beneath his grandparent's farm, had been the most happiest of his childhood.

His grandfather, after asking permission from his parents, would come with the entire fishing gear ready, and take him fishing. His granddad had been the only one, who would never 'speak down' to Milo. He'd always talked to him as to one of his closest friends and asked Milo's opinion in various occasions. He too seemed to be very wary of his son in law and Milo had sensed that grandfather tried to evade talking or even meeting him. If he had only just arrived and Milo would have wanted his granddad to stay, once father entered the front door, granddad would say that he was just leaving.

Once, mother had said that they had different views and opinions for many issues.

But grandfather had been the only one that had made Milo feel worthy of himself, however.

His parents had paid for home tutoring beside the education received at school, and although he'd been at the top of his class, the results had not seemed good enough to satisfy father. There'd been many a time while sitting to eat dinner, on those rare occasions, when his father ate with them, when his father would bring up a subject to 'test' Milo.

Milo would feel the food chocking his throat as he'd struggle to find the answers.

Then he'd sense mothers' efforts to change the subject and then his father lashing out on her yelling that Milo had inherited his stupidity from her.

Adjusting in their new place had been very hard at first as he could not speak the other children's language.

His mother wouldn't allow him mixing with them, anyway.

But fairly soon, the 'alike stony faces' that he'd seen in their old home that evening, started to show up at their new home.

It seemed that they too had moved in here.

And the 'stony alike' faces had children as well.

He had been permitted, after completing all the tasks set by his home tutor and double checked by his mother, to go out and play with 'the stony faces' children.

Walking, briskly, towards his home, he was not entirely sure if he should consider *that* 'his' home anymore.

Milo's thoughts returned to Vera.

He was 25, studying law, turned down his father's suggestion to become an army officer, which had caused them to fall out for more than a year.

Since he'd turned fifteen, Milo had spent most of the time, for one or another reason, in no speaking terms with his father.

Milo was in love with a very beautiful and intelligent girl.

Why couldn't he -make a home of his own? It was the first time that this question had sprung nudging in on his mind.

It pleased him profusely to think that Vera and he could be living alone.

Their life would be far simpler if not complicated and overshadowed, as expected, by his parents' moods and demands. But, then, he dismissed that thought from his mind as quickly as it had edged in.

How could he be an ungrateful, undutiful, child?

As the only child he was expected to never leave the parental home.

'Hang on a minute' he said to himself.

'Who ever had suggested *that* beside his father?'

Without ever pointing his finger directly at him, his father had seized every; opportunity to make his point on this subject. He had expressed his profound despise for x persons' son who'd left his parents without as much as a backward glance.

Or what an ungrateful child, one of his friend's son had been, for not thinking twice but leaving home at eighteen.

Milo felt resentment swell up.

It had been his father's imbuing way of moulding his brain and shaping his character.

He, Milo thought bitterly, *would have foreseen that if not love for my parents, my dignity, and my efforts to appear a grateful, dutiful son would keep me home.*

And it seemed that his father had succeeded, for the time being at least, as there was a high amount of uncertainty for the immediate future, specifically at that time when everything was escalating into a chaotic phase for former Yugoslavia.

****

'Ver*a*, Ver*a!*' 'Oh no, not that horrible nightmare again' Vera thought while inserting all her efforts into waking up, again.

'Vera! Vera!'
 Someone was shaking her, again.
In efforts to prevent the bright morning sun dazzle, from hurting her eyes, she opened them slowly.
Though, it did hurt her eyes, none the less.
She felt the dampness of the morning dew that had saturated her thin nightgown and penetrated onto her skin. However, the first thought to land on her brain was 'I'm free of that repulsive nightmare.'
But, the scent and a vague steam released from the earth under the morning sun spells snatched that thought away as quickly as it had emerged.
She realised that she was not in her warm bed.
 She was in the garden, under the cherry tree.
It made her sentient of what had transpired and that it had not been a nightmare.
She wished to God that the voice she'd heard were her mothers'.
But no, she'd recognised the way that their Serbian neighbour tilted her name, stressing the fourth letter instead of the second letter.

Ver*a*! Ver*a*! 'Thank God you're okay' some restrained happy notes audible in her tone.

Vera turned her head in the voice's direction and looked blankly on her neighbours face. Her gaze resembling one issued to a perfect stranger.

'They have not disturbed you, because you're their kind!' Vera wanted to yell at her, though there was no need as it was written all over in her face expression.

'Where is my mum?' Vera asked irately instead.

Grada said nothing for a moment.

Then, as if not realising that an answer was expected of her she started cursing VJ, Yugoslavian army. She went on and on, it felt hours for Vera, ranting and raving in her limping Albanian.

Her curses included all the afflicters of such atrocities upon 'poor people who did nothing more than go on about their businesses.'

She averted her eyes, casting sideway glances upon Vera all the while she spoke. Fear, panic, and ignominy mingled in her tone. Although seemingly calm now 'she's been crying' Vera gathered, tearing her gaze way from her neighbour's red rimmed eyelids and tear stained face.

'They've turned into beasts' she carried on ranting.

'As if for the first time' Vera thought to herself, trying hard to blank her neighbour out.

'They stab people, they rape, and they kill. Oh God, they burn' the last word reminded Vera of the stench smell repugnant in her nostrils. Only burnet human flesh could fill the air with such acrid smell.

She assumed that it should be from Ademi family, the nearest house next to theirs.

The two Ademi brothers, Besnik and Mirian, lived together in a big family. They had seven children between them, plus their two wives and their two old folks. It seemed that the bomb, she'd heard the blast and felt the great earth shake, had landed upon their house.

It had killed the big family and set the house aflame. The fire would've gobbled up anyone who'd have survived the blast. Vera's best childhood and teenage friend, Lena, included. Lena was Mirian's oldest child.

Vera's heart, already in pain by the early morning events, ached even more at the knowledge of her friend's and her family's sure death.

'Oh GOD, are you there, how can YOU allow such monstrosities?'

Vera caught the last sentence released from her neighbour's mouth.

She looked at Grada.

Her head tilted backwards, facing the sky. Her eyes meant to seek God's answer from the above, met nothing more than a small shredded part of the sky, as much as the thick cherry branches would tolerate.

Vera had not moved from where she'd fallen.

'Where-is-my-mother?' she reiterated the question, shouting, stressing the words one by one.

Her words, tinged with unconsumed anger, resembled slingshot hurled stones.

Grada shook at her question, looked around as in great need to disappear somewhere, to avoid answering that question.

'Your mother is dead' she lamented.

Vera's heart skipped a beat.

Although, judging by the morning events she'd predicted the answer, she'd had to ask.

'It is hope; after all, that keeps people alive.

Hope is where people cling tightly onto in order to survive through shocking ordeals' Vera told herself.

Grada's four word sentence viciously grinding the hope pressed the young heart into a heavy bleed.

'You ought to keep strong for your brother', Grada added slowly between long sights; ready to break in tears again.

Her brother's mention reeled her back into her senses, or part of her senses, anyway.

She remembered her silent promise to her mother that she'd look after her brother.

Now, with her mother dead and a father, probably dead as well, for all the knowledge of his whereabouts, she was the only family left for Joni.

Vera tried to force herself up.

Found it very difficult, as her whole body was hurting from the fall.

She fell backwards, exactly in the same spot that she'd tried to vacate.

Her injured body had rejected the command issued by the brain.

Grada offered help extending a hand towards Vera.

Vera stared it down forlornly.

She did not know what she felt at that precise moment.

Was it anger, hatred, retribution or was it fear to touch that hand.

'Serbian hand' she thought in a bitter anger.

Her thoughts lucid on her face expression.

To her it was that kind of hand that had inflicted such pain and a possible slow death upon her mother.

She stared at the stretched arm and hand again.

Slowly, as in slow motion movie, Vera witnessed the transformation of Grada's hand into a snake head.

She blinked shoving off that image, which she was sane enough to know that her mind was trying to play tricks on her.

'Given the circumstances any mind would play tricks' Vera thought favouring another look over the offered hand.

A small pistol aiming at her replaced the snakehead in the same slow motion.

'Have I taken leave of my senses?'

'What is happening to me?' she asked herself distraught by the sudden mind visions.

Then in slow motion, fearing what she may observe there, Vera dragged her gaze from the 'pistol' upon her neighbours' face.

Their eyes met.

Deep grief and motherly care was all she could read in Grada's eyes.

Then, Vera slowly, lowered her gaze upon her hand again. The snakehead and pistol had vanished. A worn out from age and hard work hand, hung in there, waiting for Vera to make up her mind.

Vera raised her own hand, slowly, allowing herself time to accept the fact that the hand offered represented nothing more than kind help.

And she was in great need for such help. She'd just lost her mother, in the most horrid unimaginable way.

Vera took hold of Grada's hand feeling the tight grasp of her small but strong hand. It was the same clasp that she used to feel when she was a little girl, and needed a lift in the air to escape the small puddles on their way back from the fields or the school.

Most of the time, Grada walked Vera and her son Vasil to school. She'd hold Vera in the air for a few seconds and the three of them would turn and look at the puddles pleased and smiling that her shoes were kept clean. For Grada and her son knew how upset Vera would be if she stained her shoes. Grada and Vasil would look at each other and then laugh at the way that Vera kept up with her appearances.

'Just like her grandmother' Vera had overheard her mother comment, apparently after she'd been told by Grada how Vera would cling onto her to escape muddy patches on their way to and from school.

And they both had laughed a hearty laugh.

Her mother's laugh echoed in her ears, welling up the first tears for her loss.

Fat slow tears, like heavy summer raindrops that come a bit too late to quell earth's thirst, began rolling down quietly. Grada still holding Vera's hand knelt down slowly, with her eyes on the ground. She daren't stare on Vera's face.

'I aven't done notink wrong and I still feel guilty' Grada thought for herself.

She longed to give Vera a warm motherly hug, but she settled for stroking her hand gently, without looking up.

After a while, Vera remembering Joni again, and with Grada's help managed to haul herself onto her feet.

She felt that her left shoulder was numb emanating a chilling ache following her left arm movements. Ignoring the physical twinge as much as she could, she wobbled towards the house. Just as she was about to step inside, Grada released her right arm, by which she'd been supporting her walk, and stood in front of her, barring her way in.

'Please don't go in!' the beseeching look more than her words brought Vera to an abrupt stop.

'Do not go in' she pleaded with Vera.

'What they've done is unimaginable, soulless, merciless bastards' she resumed her raving once again.

Vera had managed to tune her out.

Vera stretched her neck to bypass Grada and afford a peek over her mother's body.

Everything had unfolded itself like a horror, bloodbath movie. The worst fears she had when parting with her mother early that morning, had materialised. She saw nothing of her mother as her body had been covered with a blue quilt. Vera recognised it as one from Grada's house. It was the nicest quilt she had and with it she had covered her husband's body.

That quilt drawn out from the chest where she treasured the small amount of her husband's belongings, conveyed a great message to Vera.

It told her that Zana had been a very good friend and neighbour to Grada. And indeed she had been, by all means.

Grada had come as a widow with her only son just four at the time. Her husband, one of Vera's father best journalist friends, had died in a car crash. Rumour had had it that the crash had been authorised and monitored by Serbian authorities against one of their own. They saw him as a traitor just because he'd maintained his views against violence and suppression over Kosovo population. The authorities had hinted that something bad could happen to him if continued to take 'their side'. But he bravely had kept speaking his mind. Besimi had found him still alive at the hospital. He'd managed to say with great difficulties in breathing:

'Please look after my son and my wife, do not let them die from hunger.'

He'd passed way with his eyes open.

Besimi had never forgotten that beseeching look in his friend's eyes when he had, very gently, pulled his eyelids shut.

And looked after them he had.

After consulting his wife and father, he'd moved Grada from the city where she could not pay the rent anymore. They, Grada and her son would have starved after the household's breadwinner was gone. He'd brought them to a small house they had built for Grada and her young son. They provided her with a small portion of land as well. With their help she had managed to make a decent life for her son and herself. Over the years she and Zana had become like sisters. They had helped one another with the kids and the farm. Vera had grown to like her as her best auntie.

Vera caught sight of her brother lying down next to their mother's body. A new tremor of shudder was released from Vera's body.

Had he died as well? When did he come out of the 'safe place'? He had his face hidden in his mother's chest.

Oh no God don't let this be true, tell me that he is alive.

Grada noticed that a new wave of paleness wash over Vera's face. She turned slowly to see if she'd left any part of Zana's massacred body uncovered.

'Oh where on earth did he spring from?

He wasn't here ten minutes ago.'

She darted across the room and took hold of Joni. She brought him slowly onto his feet.

Vera rushed towards him.

'Thank god you're okay!' she exclaimed with her arms wide open for a tight and dear embrace.

Joni did not shift neither his arms nor face expression. Hugging him resembled that of a wooden chair being hugged for all the effort he made.

His swollen eyelid rims suggested that he'd been crying.

Vera looked straight into his eyes.

They were expressionless.

She read nothing in them, neither fear nor grief.

It seemed that soon after Vera had left the safe place he'd come out. The shot guns and close by random bomb blasts, had terrified him. He'd looked for his mother to regain some sense of comfort and security.

Apparently at that moment he wasn't able to distinguish the difference between the reality and a nightmare. He did not know whether their mother was dead or sleeping.

That sudden frightening occurrence seemed to have played havoc with his young brain, disabling it into taking in distinctive moments of the reality.

'Vera! Joni!' They heard someone calling and for a split second Vera thought it was their father.

'Oh thank God you're okay' Azemi, their father's cousin, from a first line of cousins, came in. Relished happy notes at the sight of Vera and Joni standing were obvious in his face.

The look in their faces froze the following words in his lips. Vera turned her eyes down on her mother's body, slowly, as if saying: we're not okay, look what's happened.

Just then Azemi noticed that a body was under a blue quilt on the floor.

There was no need to ask, he just knew.

'What, just what on earth is *she* doing here?' he demanded indignantly meaning Grada.

It seemed that all the anger and sorrow that he felt for Zana and her senseless demise was going to spill out over the Serbian neighbour.

Carelessly, he put his butt rifle on the floor and leaned on it like an old man on his cane. Zanas' death had coerced a heavy weight upon his shoulders.

The question hung in the air and no one had answered yet.

Vera, while her brain was slowly 'downloading' this new situation, managed to work out as to whom that bristly *she* belonged to.

Slowly, as in a trance, she gazed down at the rifle.

Would they, my father and his followers, turn their guns upon innocent Serbian women and children too?

Are they trying to match the destructive, atrocious, force of the soulless beast, let out from its ancient cave?

If so I would want nothing to do with them.

She had not realized that she had been voicing her inaudible thoughts, until she heard Azemi say:

'Hey, hey, slow down, I'm not going to kill anyone.

But at this moment I don't want to see any of their kind' he concluded penitently.

Then kneeled down slowly, and lifted up, just a little, the quilt to see Zana's face.

The swift replace of the quilt where it had been, warned Vera that what he'd seen had terrified Azemi.

She longed to touch her mother's body.

Azemi, hearing her approach, dartingly, barred her way.

'Vera, please, no!' he said, roughly pushing the rifle on the floor and hugging her.

From his pleading look, Vera contemplated that he would rather want her to remember Zana's face as it always had been: smiley, kind and beautiful.

Not what the insipid monsters had made out of her face.

Azemi was having difficulty in swallowing his own grief and guilt.

What was he to say to Besimi, when he went back to the mountains?

He'd volunteered to go back in their village.

Being fully aware of the very tangible dangers had not impeded his decision. He'd planned to organise evacuating the villagers from their homes up to the surrounding hills and mountains. Get them in hiding for the time being. But the paramilitary forces had been quicker. When he'd heard the first bomb blast from a great distance, his heart had sunk. He'd realized that he had been too late in his rescue mission.

And he felt terribly guilty, although he'd done his best to reach the village in time.

The paramilitary bastards had beaten him to it.

But they had tanks and army vehicles and perhaps the intelligence of paramilitary forces dispatched towards the surrounding villages had reached people too late. They had been quicker than his swollen sore feet.

'That is a poor excuse to feel less guilty' he told himself harshly. What was he to tell his badly wounded friend and commandant? That Serbians had been there, ahead of him. And would he ever be ready to tell him what they had done to Zana.

Her charred face came into his mind's eye once again, as he last saw it.

Her left eye was not in its socked.

A pool of coagulated blood levelled the empty hole. The torn bottom lip hung over her chin, while a deep line that cut through her left eyebrow and nose reached to the right ear.

The line, wide enough to get through his little finger, like the eye socked, was filled with coagulated blood that was still leaking, slowly, at the end, near the right ear.

While holding Vera, tight, in desperate efforts to level her out of these tormenting moments that seemed to have engulfed her, Zana's face appeared in his view, as it once was; beautiful, kind and caring.

Since she'd come to their village, as Besims' wife, Zana, in some ways, seemed to have replaced his sorely missed elder sister. She'd married and moved to America.

He had been seven years old at that time and had never seen his sister again.

'There'd be loads of paper work before she sets foot in Kosovo again,' her Kosovo-American husband had revealed to their family. The phone had been the only mean of communication from then on. Azemi had sensed on Zana the same caring and kindness soul that only his sister had seemed to possess. And he'd taken to her, turning on her doorstep with the smallest scratch on his kneecaps caused by his mischievous deeds.

She'd plaster his knees, stroke his hair and give him biscuits or sweets which were a real treat back then.

And she was never empty handed. Nobody really knew how everything lasted longer in her hands. All the village children had loved her. She seemed to sense their needs. Sometime they needed only a little bandaging while sometimes they needed some attention and affection that their very busy mothers had failed to provide.

And that extremely good soul's body, with a hardly recognisable face, lay lifelessly on the floor.

He leapt back to the reality thinking that there was not enough time for sentiments and grief, if he was to do something for the remaining members of this family.

Just then he noticed that Grada had slipped quietly out of the room, while Vera and Joni were still, wide eyed standing. Judging by their pale faces and hollow stares, the shock of their mother's completely and utterly unnecessary death, was still working its way in sinking in with them.

****

'They might come back, and kill whoever survived the first wave' Azemi said tersely to Vera. She was still standing, with a vacant stare. He wanted to shake her out of that trance she'd fallen in and she was not making any efforts to rupture.

'We need to be on our way out of the village as quickly as we can' he added tetchily.

Azemi wondered if they, the paramilitary forces, had taken east and arrived at the next village and killed his two old and fragile parents who were staying with one of his aunts.

'Does anyone know what direction they took when left from here?' Azemi asked Vera who was still standing with that frightening hollow stare.

'Come, you need to get out of here,' he pulled her lightly from her hand.

She did not move.

Slowly she turned to look at her mothers' body, lying on the floor.

'I will bury her body and catch up with you.

You need to go out and see who else has escaped death and gather together to hide in the mountains' Azemi said while pulling her and Joni outside. He walked towards the shed where he knew he'd find the tools needed to dig Zana's grave.

At that moment Grada and her son Vasil, entered from the main gate.

She was holding a small battered leather bag.

'Allow us to do that for her' Grada said directing Vera who was standing and seemingly in no fit state to take any decision.

'I bet you can't wait' Azemi said hissing through his teeth.

'Let them!' the voice came out, unexpectedly, quite strong, from Vera.

'Did you see which direction they pursued after leaving our village'? she asked them ignoring Azem's protests to leave Zanas' body in their hands.

'They're headed west, towards Prepa' Vasil answered meekly.

'Oh no!' Azemi thought of the teacher's gathering for one of their annual meetings there.

He knew that there was nothing that he could do, just hope that they'd have been alerted in time to cancel meetings and even cancel teachings.

'*Hope against hope*' he thought to himself helplessly.

'Quickly get some food and clothes, anything you can carry on your back and get ready to hit the road' he said to Vera.

He shot an angry look at Vasil and his mother. It translated to, '*You bastards, you got your own way*' and strode way.

'*He is going to find out who else has survived and organise their evacuation, or at least try to organise* a *pitiful evacuation*' Vera's brain made the first small steps of returning to reality.

She went upstairs to see if she could grab some of Joni's and her clothes, remembering the backpack that her mother had prepared and given to her that horrible early morning.

She could not go back and fetch it from the hiding place.

It would be more time consuming.

When Vera reached Joni's room was startled by the unexpected state the room was in. Clothes were strewn all over the room. All chest drawers were open and all their contents were either on the floor or half on the floor, half hanging.

Everything was upside down.

She was not able to tell whether anything was missing or not.

She found a pair of jeans and a woolly jumper which she gathered would be useful for Joni to take with them.

She grabbed from the floor two not matching socks and a pair of pyjamas that was hanging from a middle drawer.

While in the corridor towards her room she could not stop herself of stealing a glance through her mother's open bedroom door.

Reluctantly, she went in.

It was in similar state with that of Joni's.

The only difference was that she could instantly identify missing items which were her mother's jewellery and her fathers' ivory smoking pipe, which he'd never used. It had been a gift from his grandfather.

A big hole on the wall replaced an enlarged wedding photograph of her mum and dad which had camouflaged the small safe.

It had contained all family's budget.

She stroked tenderly one of her mother's favourite dresses and then thought of taking it with her. It would be something from her mother.

'Who knows if I'll ever come back?

The future is as bleak and uncertain as the turbulent water torrents in heavy rain winter days' she thought discordantly.

She left her parent's bedroom and went in hers.

Same view but she was past caring by then. She did not even try to scan the room for missing items.

Looting seemed to be another point beside killing and rape in the paramilitary's agenda. She grabbed a few items from the floor which she thought could be useful while living in mountain caves. Hurried downstairs.

She crouched down, placed her knees near her mother's head, and held her breath for a few seconds.

Terrified of what she might see she did not lift the quilt. She bent forward until her lips touched her mother's covered forehead. She kissed it lightly and clambered back on her feet saying in a trembling voice that tore through her heart,
'Goodbye Mum.'
Once out, she caught sight of Joni sitting quietly on granddad's old wooden bench. It was near the shed and she remembered her granddad smoking the pipe there when he was too old to help around the farm.
Grada and Vasil had all the tools needed to dig, but it seemed they were standing expecting something from Vera.
 She could sense an air of expectancy hanging around, however she could not fathom what was expected of her now.
She looked questioningly at Grada. She spoke hesitantly.
 'We were thinking to bury her in your garden, under the cherry tree, not at the village cemetery' Grada stated sounding not sure that this was the best idea.
 'Do whatever you think it's best. You know better than anyone else what mum would've wanted' Vera added and did not fail to notice from their face expressions some sense of relief that her words brought to Grada and her son.
 They, in some peculiar way, comprehended that Vera did not hate them. And they were happy for that, as happy as they could be under these dreadful circumstances.
Reasonably she shouldn't hate them.
It would not make sense.
But, what was making any sense that day?

'Come on Joni we ought to go' Vera said softly taking her brother's small hand in hers. He scrambled on his feet. Grada noticed that he had no shoes on.

'Wait!' she said to Vera and hurriedly disappeared inside.

When she came out she was holding two pairs of trainers. Apparently, the small size, were Joni's and the bigger size were Vera's.

Vera noticed mud on their feet but did not care.

She slid her feet in the shoes and did not bother herself with the laces, while Grada had gone down on her knees doing Joni's shoe laces.

Vera pulled her brother lightly when his laces were done, and started towards the gate.

Grada picked the leather bag she'd been carrying when she came, and put its handle in Vera's hand.

'Take it, it is not much but you're going to need it.'

She had anticipated that Vera would not even think about food, she'd brought something from her home.

Vera accepted it, reluctantly, though.

Once out of their front door, with Grada looking at them with awfully sad eyes, Vera saw Azemi with a group of people, coming towards her. She recognised all of them as from their village.

It was no more than 60 people of all ages, mostly women and children, in that crowd, from a village with roughly 450 households. That spoke volumes to her.

Men, young and old, those that had managed to escape bombing, had been pushed forcibly out of their houses and herded, God knows where. Perhaps to never be seen alive.

She quietly, pulling Joni with her left hand, joined the crowd.

'We are the leftover of this, once very lively, village' she said inaudibly to herself.

No one looked at each other's eyes.

Heads bowed down, and moaning quietly, Vera noticed that many of them had open wounds on their bodies.

They arrived at a small but clear crystal torrent.

Azemi stopped.

Anyone who had been wounded, children, and elderly folk needed pairing up with someone stronger. They needed help to keep the balance while jumping from one stone to another in the gurgling stream.

Vera was ordered to help a young man who had a gushing wound on his left thigh.

She recognised him as he had been one of her admirers. He had tried in vain to win her heart.

His wound was bleeding.

The moment he sat down to wait for Vera to come back after helping Joni to cross the stream, a small pool of blood formed beneath.

From his unbearably sad eyes Vera read the fate of his entire family.

She needn't ask.

She'd been friends with one of his two sisters.

Agnes her name was.

She had tried to play the messenger for her brother, until Vera had told her that her heart had been already set in someone else. She had been sad for her brother, but they had not broken their friendship.

Vera had known all his family members, mother father, one brother and two sisters that he had. She'd never had a chance to speak and socialise with any of them, apart from Agnes, that was.

Vera could sense that he was losing blood, and it was making him feel dizzy.

It became very difficult for her to keep him from falling into the rushing stream.

With great exertion she managed to get him dry on the other side, something she could not say for herself, however.

The last second she had to jump in the water to keep Fatmir dry, as he was about to lose his balance and fall.

Being with the crowd, among people who were suffering similar loses she felt her heart lighten a little.

Perhaps it was the help she had to provide, or perhaps it was the collective sharing that had lightened, diminutively, the burden of her loss.

They all set for the surrounding hills.

The group was being led by Azemi and two other young men, who appeared to have escaped with no wounds on their bodies. The same thing could not be said for their hearts.

Although trying hard to conceal it by offering help to elderly and women with children, the ache they felt inside had etched itself in deep lines around their youthful eyes. The inside pain had cast slightly downward tugs at the corners of their mouths. Their shoulders had stooped from the heavy burden of having to dig shallow graves for their most beloved ones.

They had aged within hours.

Just behind them came a man in his forties with his two children probably eight and ten or eleven.

Time after time he'd turn to look towards the village and quiet sobs would escape his lips.

While his sons, like Joni, seemed to register very little of the reality around them. They had glassy eyes and expressionless faces. They were too traumatised to download what was happening around them.

Later, Vera learned that that man had lost his wife and his two other children, daughter five and a toddler son.

Following closely were a group of women with children from a few months old to ten year olds.

One of them was pregnant.

She was very young, perhaps two or three years older than Vera, and very beautiful.

Vaguely, Vera recalled, her being married somewhere far. Rumour had had it that every young man in their village and the villages nearby had had a crush on her.

In the three years that Vera had been absent from the village, a lot had happened.

Apparently, the young pregnant woman, had been visiting her parents when all hell had broken lose.

There was another, young girl, perhaps Vera's age that bore a striking resemblance with the pregnant women. She appeared more refined though. Despite that dishevelled state, she was in at the moment; she was sporting the latest haircut trend.

Vera thought them as sisters, but the younger one must have been studying somewhere in the big cities.

Unlike her sister's weathered skin which told the tale of working outdoors, hers was very pale, rarely gone outdoors.

They all, with no exception, had their clothes partly or all covered in dust and soot or were, somehow, bedraggled and torn, which explained where they were coming from; absconding from ruined houses.

There were different people in that crowd. Vera looked for her cousins.

She knew.

Clearly, the bomb and the fire had left not survivors.

Vera's eyes were penetrating the crowd, scanning every face in hope of finding at least one member from the big family. Azemi, had seen her searching for them and waited for her to catch up with him.

'I'm sorry Vera! They're all dead, you have to get used to that fact.'

She knew who he was referring to, and knew the exact time when they were killed. His words had crushed that little fragile lingering hope.

'We need someone to see to Fatmir's wound' she said without permitting herself to dig further into details of their deaths.

She had anticipated that the brittle intrepidness she was trying to build around herself would crack if she was told, as she assumed she would; The big house had served as the grave of her all her closest cousins including Lena.

'Once we reach the 'Wolf's Cave' he'll be seen to by a doctor. He's losing blood, but I don't think his wound is life threatening,' he concluded and walked way swiftly. He had to reach the front again.

Vera thought of stopping and attempt to do something about slowing down the bleeding.

With what though?

She had never thought of taking with them her mother's first aid kit.

'Everything needed would have been there,' Vera thought cursing herself for not having considered the need for it.

She could sense that Fatmir was under agonising pain.

He was dragging, his left leg.

He left a trail of blood behind.

She walked out of the road, pulling Fatmir and Joni with her, to allow others to walk on.

From his torn out jeans Fatmir's fresh gashing wound was clear to see. He had been near enough from the place where one of the bombs had exploded. A fragment of metal had lodged itself into his thigh, shredding it badly in the process. It needed something tied tightly around the wound to at least slow the bleeding. She dug in her bag and found nothing suitable enough except her mother's smooth fabric dress.

'No, not that!'

She heard him say which prodded her to decide quickly. If she managed to alleviate the bleed, it meant that even dead, her mother could help other people.

'Steady yourself, it will hurt a little more, while I'm bonding it' she said in haste. She tore up the pretty dress in long strips. Vera wrapped up two wide strips around the wound, observing his face change colour in accordance with her hand movements.

Very soon they joined the tail of the group.

It was a difficult walk for him.

But he seemed to feel a little better.

Vera looked up at the sun and endeavoured to estimate the time that they might reach the hills.

The sun was up at its peak suggesting it was midday.

'We might be there within two hours' she wasn't sure as she'd never been there.

She'd seen the snow-capped, big mountain, where she presumed the cave would be, from a distance, but never been there.

She could hear the wounded moan quietly, while many others sobbing.

An infant, only a few weeks old, in her mothers' arms, started crying.

Obviously, it was hungry.

Vera had heard her mother say to other women that if a nursing mother had a big shock there would not be breast milk for days.

Suddenly, a distant bang to rapidly be followed by a series of others caused the whole group, acting as one, to come to a standstill. The distance would not disguise the type of the banging or the direction it was coming.

In a few seconds everyone worked it out for themselves.
The village perched at the foot of the mountain, they desperately intended to reach, was being shelled by the Army artillery. They had to cross a river going over the Long Bridge and all the way through the village that was being shelled, to reach their mountain destination.
Now what!?
Nobody asked the question but it hung in the air like a dark cloud.
All eyes turned towards the three leaders.
Azemi left the road and went a few steps back beside it.
Found a stone and hoisted on it.
Everyone turned on their right locking him in their gaze to listen for a solution.
All, except the hungry infant, had silenced their sobs and moans subsequent of physical and heartache, and were looking intently at Azemi.
All knew him and trusted him but this new situation seemed with no solution.
They could not return, as they were told that other batches of other paramilitaries would be released to fork the villages for survivors.
And, they could not go on.
If they did, it seemed that they'd go straight 'from the frying pan into the fire'.
Azemi, bowed his head for a few seconds, which seemed an eternity for Vera who was holding her breath with laboured efforts. She did not want to miss anything that he'd say.

'I think- he started –that we continue until we reach the river… - A collective gasp rippled through the crowd, interrupting his speech.

'Hear me out! It is what I think is best. Then if anyone has any better suggestion let's hear it too' he added a little annoyed for not being able to finish quickly.

They all knew how precious every minute was.

However their collective gasp wasn't unjustified.

They were terrified to go near and experience once again what they were trying to escape.

'After we reach the river, he continued, -we take a left turn upstream, until we reach 'Ura e Keqe' (Bad Bridge). There we cross the river.'

It seemed a sound plan but Vera thought that it had its drawbacks.

'But that bridge it's not likely to hold' someone from the crowd countered voicing fears of everyone.

'I was coming to that -Azemi said concentrating on what he was about to explain once again. We'll have to cross the bridge one at a time. It has been quite some time that nobody has walked over it and we don't know how rotten its wooden legs are. It is just a risk that I think it's worth taking' he concluded.

A wave of murmurs spread around.

Then with no need for any command the murmur died down.

'We think- an old man spoke for everyone -that is the only option left for us. Lead the way young man' he completed leaving no door open for auxiliary speculations.

As they neared the river, the sound of the continuous shelling, became stronger. It tallied to the amount of fear they all were already feeling.

When they reached the river the whole group came to a halt. Then Azemi motioned to follow. Instead of crossing they took a left turn and continued along the river bank, following the old, long route.

That turn had added more than a few miles to their entire strenuous journey.

Drained, exhausted hungry and frightened they reached the old flimsy bridge. It seemed that after the new, strong, bridge had been build, people had nicknamed the old one 'Bad Bridge' to warn people of its very rotten and unsafe state. Even the ropes crossing its entry were disintegrating, almost to the point of breaking.

Azemi hold up his hand soliciting quiet and permission to speak from the group. When they all, including the infant, it seemed that all that wailing had tired him out and he'd fallen asleep, became silent he said; 'I will cross first. I will listen to every crack released, and come back doing the same. When I come back we need a line with children at the front women and elderly next. While all the others, injured and otherwise, at the back'.

The old man, the one who'd spoken supporting Azem's decision to take that option, raised his hand.

'Yes uncle Adil'? Azem provided consent on the group's behalf.

'I think we, elderly should stay at the back. And if we are not able to cross we'd be pleased that we did something for the younger generation. Moreover, I do not think that they are out to kill old people, so we should be pretty safe to return' he added sure that all the old folk were thinking the same.

'I for one do not agree with you -Vera amazed even herself when she directed the old man. We all know and you especially what they, the Serbs, have been and obviously, still are capable of doing. I think we'll stick with what Azem said' she stated ignoring the old man's protests for listening to a 'child' as he said referring to Vera.

Azemi regarded the group expectantly, and when no one tried to provide any other suggestion, he made for the bridge.

He removed the ropes and walked slowly over it.

Everyone held their breath.

The little creaks and cracks sunk in the rivers' drone.

Nobody heard anything, but Azem felt the tremble of the wooden planks as he stepped on them.

He came back.

And the first to go over the bridge was the woman with the infant in her arms. He'd been crying for the best part of that ghastly journey.

Every time one person went over the bridge people on both sides would hold their breaths terrified that the bridge would give way.

Vera was the last to step on it.

It seemed that it was stronger than people had thought it would be.

'Perhaps God has not abandoned us completely' the old man muttered looking at people around him.

'Au shush, just shush' the old women next to him, apparently his wife, directed him tetchily, annoyed of his unnecessary interferences. In her eyes he had caused the group to waste precious time.

By the time they all were on the other side of the river, the sun had gone down west. Within two hours it would set and the air would get chilly.

No one was properly dressed to ward off the chill of the coming evenings.

Within half an hour, Vera estimated, they would reach their destination, *'provided we don't need to avert direction again'* she thought inaudibly, fearing that they might have to, again. Once at the top of the last hill, before the mountain they had to start climbing, she glanced back, as if for the last time, at their distant village.

Wisps of thick smoke from the burning houses, coiled in the air crafting a dark grey cloud of smoke where they met, coming from all directions. Beyond that grey cloud, the setting sun with its deep scarlet, laced in yolk streaks of rays, had painted the horizon in blood red.

Vera felt her heart, ache and her legs wobble.

But she couldn't give up. There was Joni. Who would he have if she succumbed to sorrow?

There were many others who had lost every other member of their family.

Fatmir was one of them.

She had her brother, and her father was somewhere in the mountains.

Azem had told her so.

She willed herself to carry on and try to provide a helping hand for those who were worse off physically and emotionally. There was one thing she could not come to terms with, though.

Why all this should be happening?

She'd asked herself that question for the umpteenth time.

Quite a while back, she'd heard her father comment: *'Some politicians can, as history has proved, brainwash an entire nation.'*

She could not bring herself to believe that all the killings, rape and loot that the Serb paramilitary was carrying out, was the will of the entire Serb nation, the entire mass of ordinary people.

She'd read loads about how they, all Balkan nations assembled their armies and fought off the Ottoman Empire.

While she knew, did not need to read, that despite the last past hundred years of bloody past, Albanians and Serbians had learned to live alongside each other. After the Second World War, while Tito had been in power, communication between the two cultures had improved greatly. People used to live in harmony and respect each other's culture diversity.

However, last Serbian president's arrival had seen the 'communication' building crumble down.

Disseminated fragments and specks of that crumbling building were hurled way as jails were filled with Albanians. Unemployment had hit the highest rates to compensate for those who remained out of prisons.

But, she would never have thought that it all would have to spiral out of control like that.

She had thought that the world was too civilised to slip back to an analogous 'Nazi', past.

At last, after that long march, Vera noticed that the leaders had reached a dense copse of trees. Tthe path, they were hoofing on, vanished under the trees.

All the way up she had a niggling thought at the back of her mind. They might have been followed by Serb paramilitaries.

She could not help peeking over her shoulder, time after time, to check.

Vera was exhausted both emotionally and physically. First pangs of hunger were tugging at her belly. At the thought of being more sheltered once in the thick cluster of the tall shadowy pine trees, she felt some sense of relief sip through her badly distressed brain and exhausted body.

She stopped at the base of a large pine tree. And turned, flinging a last fleeting look, just before she'd disappear into the woodland. She blinked twice to make sure her distraught brain and tired eyes weren't playing tricks on her. Within seconds the sense of security and relief build by reaching the woods, deserted her. She felt her legs buckle as her body went limp with fear.

******

Milo reached the front door and rushed inside.

He went over in the dining room.

It felt cold, despite the warm spring day, outside.

It had felt like that for years.

His fifteenth birthday came flooding his memory.

That day he'd felt cold and lonely than ever.

'Something equal to what I'm feeling today' he thought aloud.

His mother had asked him to run some errands for her on the day before his fifteenth. On the way back he'd thought of giving his father a surprise by appearing unannounced at his office door.

'I'm his son' he'd said escaping the reception girl who had tried barring his way.

He had swung open the office door with all carelessness that being fifteen supplies a person with. His innocent, happy smile at the thought of giving his father a pleasant surprise had been replaced by a disbelieving repulsed grin.

For a slight moment he'd been rooted to the spot.

His father, with his back to the door, charged up with adrenaline and trousers around his ankles, had scarcely noticed that the door had been flung wide open.

On his office table lay a blonde woman.

Milo could clearly see his father's veins, on his gleaming from sweat red neck, throbbing as he, animal like, propelled himself inside the blonde.

She, completely naked, had her face to the wall.

She'd slowly turned her face; training the gaze on Milo.

Her tear stained face mirrored the deep suffering of her soul and body.

She did not bother to even move or make any gesture of panic at being caught in the act.

She'd seemed relieved and hopeful that Milo's presence would free her from the torment moments she was going through.

Following the blonde's gaze his father had turned partially, without stopping, to face Milo.

He seemed so unfazed by a third person's presence as if what he was performing in his government office was the most normal thing to do.

'What are you doing here?

Get out and shut the door' he'd hissed, anger seething through his teeth, shooting a fuming look through his bleary red eyes.

He gave the blonde, who tried to vacate the table, a hefty shove, warning her to stay put.

He had no intentions of permitting himself to be interrupted, even from his son, who until then had had no idea what kind of a monster he'd been blessed with for a father.

His mother had wrapped him in cotton wool and protected him from the severe reality of his father's degraded life.

The blonde had winced from pain as the back of her head had thwacked the wooden table, and gone quiet.

She knew who she was dealing with.

She'd had to give in to his demands as he'd threatened to kill her husband and their two year old son.

When she'd tried to leave the job, she'd witnessed a deliberate accident, another car bumping into theirs and about to jostle them out of the motorway. A quick phone call made from her mobile phone to her boss, had saved her family from a gruesome death.

From then on, this was one of the smallest tasks she had to perform for him.

He had told her that should she try to escape, by leaving town, he'd find her and kill all her family.

She knew he wasn't bluffing.

When her arrangements failed to provide, what he really pined for, he, incensed, would take it out on her by raping her savagely. It seemed that was exactly what he'd been doing when Milo had walked in on him. And all the workers knew, including the reception girl, but didn't dare speaking out.

They all were aware of one of their colleagues, disappearance, once she'd spoken out and reported him to their superiors. They, the superiors had done nothing and the girl, within a few days had vanished.

Nobody dared to ask questions.

Milo's father had established his vile reputation.

Milo had needed a few moments to digest the situation he'd found himself in. Sensing that he was witnessing a rape enraged him.

He stepped in fully and grabbed his father from behind, from both arms and pulled with all the strength he could muster. Caught off guard, he was pulled back easily. But with the adrenaline levels already at the highest peak, had recovered his senses very quickly, flinging a strong right which had connected tightly with Milo's left jaw.

It had sent him sprawling across the floor and through the door. Milo had landed on the offices' door step.

His shameless father had bent down and picked his trouser belt, pulled up his trousers, so as not to prevent him from booting Milo out.

And kicking the door shut, this time, he'd locked it.

As the key had turned in, drilling through his brain, Milo had listened, for a while, to that woman's quiet sobs.

His father had resumed his puffing and groaning. He had been louder with his growl sounds, bearing resemblance with a hyena scavenging on its prey.

Milo had shuffled himself from the floor.

His jaw had gone completely numb, but he'd felt his heart far more dead than his jaw.

He had dragged himself out of the building, deflecting the reception girl's questioning and frightened look.

He'd arrived home, dishevelled and angry.

He had known that his father had a cold heart, long ago. That day Milo had been convinced that his father had a cold black stone for a heart.

His mother had asked him if something had been wrong and he'd spilled it all out.

He had been even more baffled at his mother's; palpable, 'know it all, son' look. Although she'd made efforts of hiding it, Milo had got the clue.

She had known and done nothing about it.

That's how she'd been all her life, as long as Milo could remember, going around the house like a shadow. Finding nothing more important to occupy herself with, she had turned housekeeping into an obsession. And it seemed that little else could attract her attention.

Milo had felt anger with a twinge of pity raise from the depth of his heart towards his mother.

He'd gone to bed without dinner that night, but found it difficult to sleep.

Late, when he'd been about to drift into a disturbed sleep, he'd heard the key turn in the main doors' key hole. He'd heard his mother talk, he could not make out what she was saying, but his father's indignant replies had been crystal clear for Milo.

'Why did he come there?

I really want to give him a good belt' he'd added going off to bed.

Then he'd stopped halfway, in the corridor, Milo could hear him even better.

He'd said 'I do not want to know what you and him do, but I want a perfect birthday for him.'

With that last growl he went off to bed, one he did not share with his wife. They had years that had slept in separate rooms, as long as Milo could remember.

That night, Milo, had considered leaving home, but where to. He could not afford renting.

His mother had said to him, her voice trembling, that she had provided her husband with permission to do anything he wanted, because she couldn't sleep in the same bed as him.

When asked why she'd tossed at him some answers that had left Milo even more confused. One of them had been that she had some kind of disease, not convincing as Milo knew that she had seldom seen the doctors. And she feared that it might be contagious and her husband would catch it if he slept with her.

Many people had come for his fifteenth birthday; they had been invited already. It had been the last as Milo had not wanted his parents to play happy families in front of their friends and relatives.

It had been just as well for his father.

He'd said to anyone who'd been listening that Milo hated birthdays.

'Just like his father' he had concealed his chat in front of Milo.

'We couldn't be more different' Milo had thought aloud. His father, ignoring Milo's muttering remark, had hastily changed subject.

For months they had not spoken to each other.

Sometimes there had been years, but even when they were in speaking terms, they avoided being in each other's company.

'I think I've had enough, - Milo said to himself.

I need to go and find a place to rent. Rent, rent, I've got no access to any money –and it will be a good few months before I would pin down my first job.'

He retained what his mother had enlightened him once with. His grandfather had left him some money that he could access after his 21st birthday.

He had not thought of it before.

No need to.

He'd been all his life hungry for parental loves, which even his mother, had failed to provide.

He'd never been hungry for money to spend, however.
His mother had seen to it.
Milo had never asked.
It seemed it had been a guilty conscience from her side.
He made for his father's workroom.
Mother had said that one of the inheritance copies signed by grandfather was being kept in there.
He'd rarely set foot in his fathers' work room.
It was the same as he always remembered. A sense of an unexpected and unpleasant surprise, clutched at his heart like the sharp claws of an eagle on a small frightened rabbit.
Milo entered his father's den.
That's what he thought of it 'a den.'
Milo wondered if his father had whisked in and out any of his mistresses. After that repulsive encounter at his work office, Milo had become aware of his father's string of mistresses. Memories of old unpleasant times swept aside, he looked at the large wooden shelves with a big sight of helplessness.
There were so many documents and books.
He stared on the documents on the table.
'Top secret' he glimpsed over a red covered brochure.
And just for the thrill of it as if defying his father, Milo chose to open and read in it.
'Ethnic cleansing' a strange title he thought.
He leafed through, skipping the written parts, until a map took hold of his view snatching Milo's attention.
There were Kosovo cities, towns and villages, in bold, with big black and red arrows drawn over them. He read the map

decode, underneath. Black arrows were deciphered as; force out Albanian population in any way possible, avoid killing. If happened conceal the evidence.

Red arrows, which covered around 90% of the map, deciphered; cleanse the area of Albanians by any means, killing included. In brackets 'enrich yourself in the process.'

There were five names with signatures underneath the code. His father's wasn't one of them.

A big red arrow shadowed Vera's village.

Milo's heart skipped a beat. His love for Vera and Vera's for him had seemed to compensate for all the love he had lacked since he had been born.

It was a good two hours walk if he decided to walk there. There was no doubt in his mind that he should get in her village, as soon as possible. He thought of borrowing a bike from one of his friends. But he had no idea where they were. They had not been in touch for months.

'I could go down and buy one, in the town shops' he thought.

—I'll find the money' he darted across the room, towards his father's safe. He could see that there was no way that he could have access to the safe.

In a furious rage at the thought of, possibly, not seeing his sweetheart again and his father having played a part in all that unfair business, he lashed out.

He thrashed the office.

He tore, savagely, the brochure and hurried down stairs, to find his mother standing, blocking the doorway.

She said nothing, but while moving aside, she extended an arm towards Milo. His vision had been blurred by the rage he was feeling inside, and at first he did not see that his mother was holding a big wad of money.

He stopped, feeling wrath swell inside against his mother too.

'Oh and that's how you think you make everything all right, isn't it Mum'? he contorted trying to prevent a possible spill.

'No son, do not start, hear me out first!'- She raised her voice, which surprised and commanded Milo to wait.

'For years I have hated myself for conceiving and nurturing *his*, your father's seed. My heart has ached at not being able to love you properly, because the interminable hate I have felt, and still do, for *him*, always intercepted. But there is far more to it, than you'll ever know. I had no choice and neither had the string of women lovers that he had over the years. I could not sleep with him not because I was sick, but because I felt sick by him and what he did and, obviously, lugs on doing. Soon enough you'll find out, there is no need to say anymore now. You know enough for now. Take this money son'; she said pleadingly sensing Milo's reluctance.

She took off one of her best rings, a gift from her father. Her wedding ring had been long gone.

It had not even managed to leave a mark on her finger.

'And this ring from me for your sweetheart. Find her son and never come back! I will go and spend my retirement, from the misery life with your father, with my mother' she concluded leaving Milo stunned.

Her father had died three years previously. With him had gone the father figure that he'd presented for Milo. He had spent with his grandparents all summer holidays and other short school breaks. Loved every minute of it, while, always dreading coming back.

She moved a little closer and leaned to embrace him, but sensed him stiffen and hold back for a slight moment.

Then as if what he'd been feeling for his parents' had dissipated in seconds, Milo slung his arms on his mother's shoulder in a tender squeeze.

Kissed her in both cheeks and before he would melt down and cry in tune with mother's hot rolling tears, he shot for the door. She had managed to, quietly; slip the money and the ring into his coat pocket, while he was hugging her.

Milo stopped on the doorstep as if forgotten something.

'I will find you when I come back'-he said hastily. He was aware of one thing that he greatly lacked now, time.

And that was something that he had to race against.

'You know where to find me' she said her voice wavering.

He flew out in the street and made for the big bicycle shops at the town centre.

Got there, out of breath, in a few minutes to find them all shut down.

Something, just then, clicked with him.

One of his friends, lived, used to anyhow, just few yards away and he owned a new, oh well it was new some months ago, bicycle.

In a heartbeat he found himself in his doorstep.

Mishkas' mum answered the door.

'He is not in' she skipped the polite pleasantries she used to express whenever Milo visited them.

'Actually, -he paused to compose himself and explain clearly without being rude.

'I came for his bicycle,' he managed to blurt out.

'I am in urgent need to be somewhere and it will help me to arrive in time' he said hopeful that she would not ask any probing questions.

'Of course you do, and where is that father of yours these days?' she asked notes of irony conspicuous in her tone.

Milo stiffened, bowed his head down, and swallowed hard.

That question had caught him off guard.

'If your mum had not confided in me I would have assumed that the saying "*Like father like son*" is true, but in your case, it obviously isn't.

Get in and grab the bike. I do not have the strength I used to have to carry it out for you. I can see that your feet are itching to ride and be wherever you want to be. Look after yourself son' she added while swinging the door shut.

He heard the big, rarely used, rusted bolt, crunch into place. It was still a good three hours before the night with its darkness crept in.

'*It seemed as an undeclared war is about to shoot off. And it has frightened ordinary people. As per usual, they, the ordinary people, would be made to pay the ultimate price, not those who coax the embers to blaze into a vivid fire. Some war that my father and the brainwashed 'stony faced' robots are igniting'* Milo thought indignantly.

Just then it dawned on him that he had no idea of which route to pursue, to reach Vera's village. All he knew was to start southwest out of town.

'I'll ask by-passers for directions' he told himself, unfazed.

'I'm coming sweetheart' he said lovingly as if she was a few paces way.

With no idea at what he might find and what waited for him behind those distant hills, he set off in his rescue mission.

His pure love and youth had loaned him enough courage and vigour, to carelessly, tread in the murky waters of 'in the brink of civil war nation' as he put it bitterly again about his father's cunning part in it.

He looked up at the setting sun and thought that he'd reach Vera's house with half an hour to spare before the night would wrap the earth in its blind dark fabric.

******

From the hill that they'd vacated for about ten minutes previously, two Serb paramilitary silhouettes had emerged. Vera was not sure if they had spotted the group entering the woodland. Once behind the trees she liberated Jon's hand and tried to free herself from Fatmir's arm. He'd been leaning on her for support as his strength was weakened by blood and family member's loss.

There was not enough time to alert the leaders.

They were quite a good few yards ahead.

She grabbed the arm of that pretty girl's Hanne.

She'd overheard the pregnant sister once or twice sigh: 'Oh Hanne my dear sister, look what *shkau** did to us?'

Whispering, she did not want the others to panic; explained quickly who she'd seen.

'Now, help this injured man and please do not let go of my brother's hand. He is too traumatized to notice what is transpiring around him. I will try to divert the Serbs from the groups' way by drawing their attention over myself' she concluded hastily leaving Hanne no time to react or say anything.

She had trouble tearing off her arm from Fatmir's.

'No!'

He shouted quite loud and four or five people turned to see what had coerced that shout. He'd been quiet trying to suppress the agonising pain he was feeling, but contemplating what Vera was about to undertake, had elicited an involuntarily bawl from him. He almost stumbled over trying desperately to keep his hold on Vera.

She tore away.

Vera reappeared out of the tree cover, onto the open. She did not see the soldiers and thought that they were just a few minutes away from her, at the bottom of a steep slope.

Just out of her sight. The path Vera and the other refugees, how ironic, refugee in their own soil, had trailed, divided in two smaller, narrower paths that went in two directions.

One was the one that the group was pursuing and disappeared behind the trees, while the other was about to be the one pursued by Vera to delude the possible chasers.

With no time to think for too long she trotted back until reaching the point where the interception for the two narrow paths, occurred. She could see that the other path also, cut into the woods after few yards. She decided to walk until she'd reach the entering point and wait for the paramilitary men to spot her and then, just then she'd break into a very swift run through the woods.

'If this plan works, I might have a chance, otherwise, I'm dead' she thought while her heart was beating a tattoo on her chest.

She stopped a few steps away from the trees, which were her last, rickety, hope.

There was not much of a chance that she'd manage to flee 'Kalashnikov' bullets. She crouched down, faking a look through her bag, while stealing glances over the main path, where she expected them to appear.

Vera saw the tops of their hats appear and a few seconds later both their faces came in full view.

They were talking and did not seem they were after anyone.

Vera stood upright, turned to make sure that they'd seen her, and broke in a frenzied run. Just then they seemed to have noticed her presence.

Fear seemed to have lent her wings which had translated themselves in strength and speed. Before they retrieved the image into their brains to have a second close inspection, she fled the open road and knifed through the thick dense, with branches brushing the ground, pine trees. They weren't sure of what had just been swallowed by the woodland, a human, or an animal, fox or rabbit.

They trailed the chase all the same.

Surprisingly, something she'd expected to commence, once they'd seen her, they did not take to shooting. Vera did not want to panic the already petrified and running way villagers. And draw attention for other paramilitaries to set off on human hunting.

******

Pavle had felt general's hand patting, rather stalwartly, him on the back. His ears had burned with pride that an army general was regarding him with such attention.

Pavle had been working at this prison for more than four years, promising his fiancée that once he'd saved enough they'd get married and buy their own farm.

The day of having saved enough seemed nowhere near in the horizon. Most of what he earned from his meagre wages was gobbled up by the rent and the tasteless food that the landlady cooked for her lodgers. What was left was sent up to his poor parents who were struggling to make ends meet.

When he'd seen the general's descent, like a farm turkey breast out head high, from a shiny army car, Pavle's heart had pitched with hope and excitement at the prospect of meeting someone that could help him to join the army.

He'd heard so many tales of fat salaries in the army.

He hoped for one thing though that the general would remember him.

Petar, the general, and Pavle's father had been very good friends when they were young. Pavle remembered him coming to their house, drinking and staying up very late with his father. But, lately they had drifted apart.

'Of course he would remember' Pavle had assured himself.

Nonetheless, Petar, recognised him and even made such a show about it.

Pavle was awe struck and did not know how to make sense of it all. He had expected to be recognised after he'd presented himself. But that was just as well for him. There could not be any other finer way than to be singled out as one who had connections above his diffident rank.

Petar had asked him to come and see him as soon as he'd finished with prison governors.

All that day, Pavle was told that 'the general' had no time for him, yet.

Late in evening someone came for him.

He'd been summoned by Petar.

Once inside the room where Petar had lodged, one that was reserved for high rank prison visitors, clouds of smoke dispersing towards the ceiling and a punch of strong whiff of vodka, slapped Pavle's face.

Petar swung in his chair to face him.

'Oh there you are' he stood up and shook hands with Pavle, while his other hand stroked Pavle's left arm softly, slightly gripping as he slid it down tracing the arm.

Pavle was steered down in a chair, very comfortable to the eye, but not so relaxing when he sat on it.

He felt sweat build up under his armpits.

General's hand lingering, for one minute too long, over his left arm and back of his hand, had made Pavle feel like he'd sat over a hedgehog, not a comfortable chair.

Common sense had told him that if something sounds too good to be true…... At last Petar had released Pavle's hand and gone to a in the wall build cupboard, which Pavle would have not noticed that it existed if he had not seen its door swing open.

A bottle of vodka and two small glasses had germinated in general's hand when he turned, swiftly, to face Pavle.

'So, I know that you are in very bad need of some money' he'd said boldly, with no preamble, rubbing salt in Pavle's embarrassing abrasion.

How does he know I wonder? Pavle uttered to himself.

'And I intend to make you rich, very rich indeed. But, -he raised his pointing finger fiercely, as if threatening someone; -it very much depends upon you. If you decide to join the army, then there is no turning back' - he'd added filling the two glasses with the strong liquid from the bottle.

Its pungent smell had cut sharply through Pavles' nostrils, the same way that the generals' words had scraped his brain. 'You won't be a simple soldier.

I have seen to it.

Here, he thwacked the wooden table with a handful of papers; here is the list of the people under your command. Now, drink to your new duty!'

He'd raised his glass commanding Pavle to do the same.

Pavle, reluctantly, had raised his glass, not sure how to react or say anything.

He'd sensed that something was not quite right. Just something did not quite jelly with him, but he also knew that he had not much say in it. He knew that he had to comply with whatever his superiors had decided. There was not much choice.

Submit or go back to my strip of land that could scarcely feed my poor parents. Bastards they know that as well-he told himself taking a swig from the vodka that filled his glass to the brim.

-V*ery generous with your kindness and your vodka, I wonder what the catch is. There is bound to be one*, Pavle could not stop conjecturing to himself.

'Read the names, you know them' - he'd said the last word in a nearly whisper coming closer to Pavle's ear. His bad warm breath had made Pavle pull back, slightly.

'Read, read –he'd coaxed Pavle, with a rasping voice like the wind through a bed of dead leaves in a dying out forest –then you'll know what I am talking about.'

Pavle had read the first three- four names before he'd raised his eyes to meet those of Petar.

Everything had become crystal clear to him.

When their eyes had met he could read the pleasure that Petar was feeling at the thought of torturing his recruiter. He'd lowered his eyes and read on. There were the entire city's' thugs, drug abusers who would sell their own mother for a pinch of dope, and thieves and *–hang on a minute* -he had told himself, *-these are from this prison, and they're killers.*

'No this can ….not be right, I can …, I cannot take up this offer' he'd mumbled fearing what flouting this offer, would fetch him.

'Ah! I'm afraid that's not very astute of you to opt for, and – mock regret radiating from every wrinkle on his repellent face - you've been released from the present job. You are now under my command'- Petar had concluded threateningly drawing out his nine millimetre hand gun and placed it aside on the table.

Pavle had felt that more than ever he'd needed a drink then. He had emptied his shot of vodka and placed the glass on the table.

'That's more like it, that's how I like my boys'-Petar had quickly filled him another one.

'And you know-his voice had turned into a rasping whisper again, -accidents do tend to happen, especially when people exceed the limit with strong drinks.'

He is blackmailing me he is threatening me with death. Is there anyone I can turn to for help?

He had tried to think if the prison governor would be able to help. But remembering the way all the prison superiors had reacted upon Petar's arrival conveyed a strong message to him. He was one with enormous power in his hands. They had been all eager to please him as if he had their lives in his hands.

And, 'lives in his hands', seems to be not only a metaphor. –He just proved it to me.

'Drink up sonny! That's what a real man does. And a *real* man fights for his country' he'd added drinking from the bottle.

Petar hadn't been bothered to fill his glass again, but started to drink straight from the bottle which Pavle found repulsive. Everything had been hideous that night.

He'd been bullied in signing the papers.

He'd been frightened into accepting his part into something he'd never wanted.

However, he'd found some comfort when he came to Pristina and found that one of his high school friends, Dejan, was in the same regiment too. He'd been dragged in also and in similar fashion. They had confided in each other and had made a pact between them. Go along with it until resolving a way out. In meantime they would evade any killings themselves and would try to deter the others from killing women and children.

Very soon they found that prevent the others from killing was out of question.

Petar had accepted Pavle's resignation as the commandant of all those criminals that were recruited '*to protect the country*'. *How ironic* Pavle had thought *–protect our country going out of our country.*

For him going to Pristina in Kosovo, was too far from his home and his sweetheart in Serbia.

There had been countless sleepless nights and tormenting moments. First witnessed killings had terrified him.

They, Petar had warned his commandant it seemed, knew that he was against killing, and watched him like hawks watched their prey. They were waiting for him to make the wrong move and an 'accidental' bullet would pave its way through the back of his head.

He had seen it happen to one of Dejan's friend. He had refused to kill unarmed young men and children. There had been four or five at about twelve to fourteen year olds. They'd said nothing at the scene; Pavle had thanked his god for not being asked to shoot over the unprotected crowd.

But once back to their headquarters a swift trial had taken place, concluding only those who'd witnessed the refusal present. The trial had delivered the capital punishment for 'breaching a war rule'. They were told to keep their 'traps shut' as this execution was going to be written off as UQK (Kosovo Liberation Army) deed.

Once out of their hawk eyes, Pavle had rushed for the filthy headquarter toilets. He could not wipe off the petrified look on peoples' faces when the shooting had started.

The wails of the youngest clutching at each other, echoed in his head. Then their falling onto each other and their hands slowly, as their life ebbed way, releasing the grip on each other, was played in slow motion in his mind over and over again. They'd been told to watch as the team assigned to carry out the execution, would act it out.

He had felt bile rise in his throat and thought that he'd die from the desperate efforts to conceal it. Once in toilet he felt his insides violently throwing themselves against his throat as he remembered how within ten minutes they were told to bury them.

Pushing them in the shallow grave they'd freshly dug, he'd felt that one of them was still alive. He'd used his hands, unlike his other troop members which rolled the bodies towards the grave using their feet.

Pavle could see that the young man had a gashing wound on his right shoulder. While turning him slowly on his back, to push towards the hole, he'd moaned meekly.

'He isn't more than fourteen' Pavle thought, struggling to keep himself from being sick. Pavle was terrified that they might construe that one was still alive and shove a bullet through his head and then his own head would be expecting one.

He could not tell and he could not try to save him.

Pavle had been very tense until all was over and no one had suspected anything. He'd broken down over his own filth in the headquarters toilets, and wept quietly.

He had buried a kid, *alive*!

And *that* more than anything else was very taunting for him. He could not find rest with his conscience. That night he'd sought a moment alone with his friend Dejan and decided that with the coming morning they'd leave the camp.

Go in any direction, just as long as it was way from these bloodthirsty animals carrying out these senseless, mindless killings.

Pavle could not sleep that night. As soon as he closed his eyes the young boy's face would dart into his room, scorning him harshly for being buried alive.

It would have been well past midnight when he had drifted to disturbed sleep only to wake up to a startling alarm bell. They were ordered to line up with the same urgency that they'd been asked to audience the execution of the civilian crowd.

For a slight moment he'd doubted Dejan.

Pavle thought that they were preparing another audience, his audience.

And it terrified him.

Then the young boy's face swam in his view and he could not shake it off no matter how hard he tried. For a few minutes, that he thought that Dejan had grassed his escape plan, he was thrown into that boy's shoes.

Then he knew exactly how it felt to be counting the last minutes and the seconds left of your life.

Later, when they were given marching orders, comprehending that it had nothing to do with him, instead of feeling a little relaxed, he felt even tenser. They were heading for more killing, loot, and rape and he was going deeper into it.

Once in the road he saw Dejan's ensemble trailing behind his. He hoped that they'd have a chance to exchange signals, if only to make sure that Dejan still was supporting him with what he'd planned.

Dawn had seen their march towards two villages, which sat next to each other divided only by a mile or so between them. Pavle had witnessed, even worse than anticipated, blood chilling civilian killings. Killing adorned with rape and loot.

Never in the most terrifying nightmare had he observed scenes like that. Women and girls were raped repeatedly in front of their families, husbands, and children.

At last, they, Dejan and Pavle had managed to sneak out unnoticed and here they were chasing a young girl through the pine trees. They had thought that once they'd pass the mountain and reach the city, could find a way to travel out of Kosovo and end this madness that had clawed at that bunch of thugs led by Petar.

Pavle and his friend Dejan had no idea that similar mobs of thugs were organised to carry out killings and ethnic cleansing all over Kosovo.

For them these recruited people, handpicked carefully by Petar, had lost touch with their human side.

There was nothing that they'd performed these last few days to render them as humans. Perhaps that had been the precise reason for being chosen by Petar, the absent link with human race.

They caught glimpses of her in and out of bushes. Without even saying anything to each other they had given chase, because both had realised that the girl was heading towards their camp. All they wanted was to catch up with her and make her avert direction.

'Stop'! Dejan called to Pavle.

'Can't we see that she is frightened from us? She might be from the village we left and she's bound to be horrified' he concluded trying to catch his breath.

'The path she's following will lead her to our headquarters and we know what lay in wait for her there' Pavle said through his heavy breathing from the fast pace run.

He was worried and a tad embarrassed that a girl had outrun them.

'Try calling out to her- Dejan said. She might understand that we're not bad and takes on board what we say to her.'

'O yah, what do we tell her that we've seen your brother and father being killed and we've done nothing to save them. Or shall we say that we've seen women being raped and we done nothing because we were pissing ourselves, because we're cowards' Pavle said.

His sharp sarcasm directed to himself mostly, had left Dejan open mouthed.

'Hang on a minute mate. That's not fair and you know it. We are far too small fishes in a pond to have power to change the course of these events. –What I'm pissed off at, is the fact that we're being outpaced by a young girl and we're failing to save her.'

At that moment the girl came out in an open space that the undergrowth had created. They could see that she'd managed to set a greater distance than the last one they'd seen her at. Talking had slowed them down.

'Hey!'

'Don't go that way!'

'You're going to be killed!'

'Stoooooop!'

They both called out. They were out of tune with each other and their words seemed to not make much sense.

She vanished beyond the bushes. In the next few minutes she'd be in the open stretch that would lead her straight to her death. They both felt like they'd just signed her capital punishment.

They looked at each other intently, breathing very hard.

Tacitly they understood what should be done. Their conscience, and they still had one, would not allow them to behave otherwise.

******

Vera heard them calling, but could not fathom what was being said to her. She let their words pass her and resonate on the big pine trees without even turning her head. Their words would go back echoing to them.

'Nice try you bastards' she said out loud but she knew they were too far to hear that.

In seconds she saw that the path was leading her out of the cluster of trees, and in an open stretch of landscape. Fear, already at the highest peak, seemed to mount even higher. It passed the line and she seemed to not care that much, not any more.

'There is a line within us' she thought, *'beyond it one is bound to go numb.'*

But she did not slow down.

She wanted to lose the two paramilitaries that were behaving, surprisingly, different from what she'd expected from them.

In distance she saw houses, but, because of the fast pace run, she

failed to notice that they were not normal looking houses.
They looked more of an army camp.
The sun was, slowly, dragging itself down at the far west, casting long narrow shadows of the houses and the trees. He was not pleased to have risen to the aftermath of the events happening during his colleague's the moon, night shift over the earth.
As it slid down, the sun even noticed a young girl's run that resembled that of a frightened reindeer trying with all its might to save its life.
Unable to change anything in that course of events, the sun attained a distant and indifferent deportment.
 The only thought now, buzzing in Vera's head was *'Reach the houses and seek shelter, hide, hide hide... hide.'*
The houses had disappeared from her view, just behind a hillock.
 Once behind the hill that she passed in very few minutes, she noticed another trail that joined the one she was running in. She slowed down trying to think where the other path might lead her to, if pursued in efforts to lose the paramilitaries.
One head turn in her right brought her face to face with a company of paramilitaries who had seen her already and were aiming to shoot at her.
'Run! Run even more, but you're dead anyway' she told herself as a series of shots punctuated, the growing cold, evening air. Carrying on the same path, she had no idea that she was headed towards the wasp nest. She still thought a village was lying behind the hill.

'Nearly there, nearly there,' she could hear the hiss of the bullets around, attempting to sink their steely teeth into her flesh. Although she could not hear the shots, she could smell the led and the dust sieved in the air when the bullets forked the ground as they went.

Strange what real fear could instil in people. They were not far to hear the shots screaming at her and to see their weapons vomit fire in her directions and yet she heard nothing.

She felt a great shove and a sharp strong sting in her left thigh. The immense push forced her face flat on the dusty road. In seconds someone was over her and calling:

'Cease fire!'

'Cease fire!'

Vera managed to turn on the side and could see one of the paramilitaries staring intently at her.

'It is one of the chasers' Vera gathered based on his red sweating face.

Before she could even try to get up, she was surrounded by all these paramilitaries leering at her.

'Wait, we wanted her first' shouted the red faced paramilitary.

'Since when you're into girls Pavle?' someone asked sarcasm thick in his tone.

'We did not know that you were into girls Dejan. We thought that you had a knack for young boys' another one ventured insolently.

They were all speaking at once, their repulsive remarks insulting her ears.

She wished she'd never learned that language.

Unexpectedly, they all went quiet. They moved a few paces back, creating an irregular circle with Vera in the middle. She still lay on the dust. Vera closed her eyes, for she surmised that someone of higher authority was approaching the leering crowd. She hoped that they'd decide to kill her there and then.

The prospect of having to endure great physical and moral humiliation, at the hands of those, by all accounts, animals, coerced on her the wish of a quick death.

She even wished that the bullet had pierced her heart not her thigh.

'I would have been spared all this pain and humiliation that for sure will follow' she thought to herself with her eyes closed and was amused that deep down she felt that she did not want to die. She still, in the most profound corner of her inner self, though she would not admit it to herself, hoped that somehow she'd survive this entire ordeal.

'Is she dead?' she heard a brusque voice and at the same time she felt none to gently a poke on her right shoulder blade. Instinctively, she opened her eyes. Immediately she could see that someone of higher rank was leering at her too. He was looking down on her and she could feel, almost taste the contempt coming in waves out of him.

The feeling is mutual -she looked at him as contemptuously as she could from that laying position.

'Drag her to the camp' - he said without removing his foot in his heavy army boot which was still pressing on Vera's shoulder blade. 'Dress her wound and bring her to my office' he added and swiftly walked ahead.

'It didn't take him long to realise that she is pretty and decide to take her first' one of her two chasers whispered to his friend while nearing her.

'Shut up, he could hear you and.... the girl ...'

She did not get what he was saying about her as the leering jeering and rude remarks coming from all directions resumed its course once again. They both bent down to help her get up, only to be bunged angrily by another paramilitary.

'Hey, if you're still thinking that you can take her first think again. The commandant seems to like her, which is something that does not happen too often and I am going to make sure that he gets what he wants' he concluded pulling harshly on Vera's arm.

'Haven't we noticed that' one of the chasers murmured to the other but made no attempts to deter the other paramilitary from taking over.

Fear, pain and humiliation visible in her face expression, Vera felt like a wounded reindeer that had no strength to run anymore. She was trapped. From what she heard she contemplated all what lay in wait for her which made her reconsider if she'd rather be dead than go through all that.

'Can I help you Dragan?' sneered a scarred face. Disgusting desire to touch her unconcealed in the way he looked at Vera. Struggling to stop himself from taking her there and then. Something he would have done if the commandant wasn't in the way. It seemed that, commandant's desire to have her to himself first had stopped him in his tracks. The scarred face needed to postpone that for later. He was sure that he would have a chance after the commander and Dragan had finished with her. He came third in the rank, and it made sense to him that he'd be the third one to scavenge on what was left.

The commander had not needed to spell it out, because he was aware that everyone knew what he meant when he asked for someone to be fetched to his office. The one with the name Dragan barely nodded and they both, roughly elbowing Vera's former chasers out of the way, grabbed her and without permitting her into making even an attempt to haul herself onto her feet, or one of them to be precise, they started dragging her. Vera felt the pain engulfing her as her left leg went completely numb. The camp seemed quite a few yards away and Vera thought that by the time she'd get there the other leg too would be in dire need of medical attention.

They were dragging her like a rag doll. She could feel the nip as sharp stones cut her skin open while the blunt ones would send bouts of strong pain to her core and bruise her legs.

Once inside the camp her eyes caught, at the farthest corner, a group of civilians guarded by heavily armed paramilitaries. There were women and children among them, sitting on their bundles, clutching at each other in fear and trepidation. A flicker of hope perched at Vera's heart. Vera thought or distraughtly hoped that she'd be allowed to mix with that group. And if that ensued she hoped that she'd be saved of what she'd contemplated would happen, before she was killed. Killing seemed high on their cards and she only hoped that she wouldn't have to go through the humiliation before the execution.

Then her predators took a left turn and she lost the civilians from her sight. They yanked her through an open door slumping her harshly on the cemented floor of what she thought of as a doctor's room. The pungent smell, that some of the drugs released in the air, charged viciously at Vera's smell buds. The two paramilitaries overturned her and in turns harshly squeezed her breasts. She tried in vain to ward them off while distracted from sleazy laughs outside the room.

'Been followed from a persistent crowd which wants to be entertained,' Vera gathered.

'Hey Drag give her another hard squeeze for me' a drunken voice goaded, apparently irritated from being told that he could not have a go right then and there. It seemed that this was an extraordinary occasion when they'd been told that they had to wait to rape someone. Vera felt a strong twisting pinch on her left breast and almost screamed from pain, refraining herself only the last second by biting her lower lip. She did not want to give them the satisfaction of breaking her, although if truth be told, at that very moment she felt at the lowest end of the food chain.

She assumed that this was going to be a nightmare that would resonate into her brain until the day she died and that was if, she had a chance of escaping with her life. And that was a big if. They joked and laughed about while taking a bunch of keys from a nail hooked on the wall. And after dangling them in front of her eyes they went out, joining in with the others in their loud jeers and crude jokes made at her expense. When they seemed to have run out of all their nauseating vocabulary, which appeared to be extremely long, they locked the door behind them.

Vera looked around and supporting herself by the wall clambered onto her feet. She could tell that there were no broken bones but, although the wound was covered in dust, the blood was still oozing from it.
 Limping, she managed to reach the wide window, which glared at the back of the building. Perceptibly, they seemed to have invaded a school building and adapted to their taste, as an army camp. Vera tried to open the window which was jammed and could not open, unless she broke the glass.
Hitting it with her fists did zilch to the glass.
At the farthest corner over a littered table she spotted a pair of curled, doctor's scissors. She knew there was going to be sooner rather than later that they'd be coming with a doctor to dress her wound as instructed by their superior.
 Lumbering as fast as she could she got to the scissors grabbed them and while going back to the window she heard indolent voices and steps, they had all the time in the world, nearing the doctors' room.
She hit the glass with all the strength she could muster, which was not that much but it broke the glass nonetheless.
With great difficulty Vera climbed on the window sill and dived down, outside in the unknown, which could not be any worse than it already was, without thinking on what she might land upon.
Dusk had enveloped the low building and all its surroundings

with the formless shadowy cape, feeding Vera with hope of disappearing into its darkness, way from those sharp clawed, cold-blooded beasts.

******

Dusted, to the point of not being recognised even by his own mother, and highly anxious at the prospect of being too late to find Vera, Milo reached the last hill that overlooked Vera's entire village.

He stopped to catch his breath.

He glanced hastily over the village and bent down to check the tyres of the bicycle. And just then his brain managed to send a signal of the image it had retrieved for Milo to work on.

He held his breath and stood very still.

Then as in slow motion he lifted his gaze from the tyres, he did not need to lift his head to throw a second look over, what it seemed the ghost of the village. There were no more than two or three houses still standing or partially standing.

The entire village had been reduced to a messy heap of rubble. Clouds of black smoke, released from still burning houses, obscured the setting sun, making the night appear closer than it really was.

His hope of finding Vera seemed even bleaker than at the start of his laborious journey. He was at the highest peak and the road that wound down towards the village, resembled an enormous viper.

It descended sneaking right and left as if to make the hill less steep and seize itself from falling on its back.

Frustrations and despair clawed at his longing heart.

There was no short cut through where Milo could use his rusty bicycle. He wanted to ride straight down, regardless of how dangerous that would be.

Half-hearted he resumed his journey; aware that after that long climbing the bicycle was at the point of breaking down.

'I might have to continue on foot' he thought as there was nothing that could possibly prevent him from trying to find his sweetheart.

He managed to get to the foot of the hill without falling from his bicycle, and the phantom village had disappeared from his view.

Although he could tell, on the way down, that both tyres were deflating, he still kept going helped by the steepness of the hill. However, on the level, muddy road, he had to discard the bike and continue on foot.

His feet ached on touching the ground with full weight pressure on them, but he started to run ignoring the ache.

First at a slow pace run then, as his legs got used to this new way of working after a long time on riding the bike pedals, he managed to accelerate the pace.

Very soon the vestiges of the village came under his observation again.

Shortly after, a very dusty, tired, and anxious looking young man entered the ghoul village. Not a soul a sound or movement in the street. It instilled a sense of unexpected fear in Milo. He had not expected to enter a ghostly village. Weaves of strong emotion were lapping in the troubled shore of his soul. He walked on becoming more heavy hearted by the minute, looking for anything that might still be moving. The prospect of finding Vera alive was becoming an unreachable one.

Near a partially standing house, he stopped.

Left the road and entered the house's courtyard. Listened carefully, trying to still his loud beating heart, for any sound that would be released from humans. He neared the ground floor window, the only one left on the still standing part of the house.

Looked through it and, swiftly pulled back.

He was horrified!

Moved a few steps back and closed his eyes.

Blood and a heap of bodies came into his view, again.

'Who is there?' someone asked meekly.

Milo stood very still.

He was not sure if he'd heard something or his troubled state of his mind and his buzzing ears were playing tricks on him. He neared the window again, with his eyes tightly shut, and tapped lightly on it.

A very weak knock answered from the inside wall, just below the window sill.

'Is there anyone inside?' he asked as normal as he could in Albanian.

'Yes-it is, come in and help please!' the voice answered feebly.

The dusk was drawing in and very soon all the surroundings

would lose their edge, becoming unclear to the eye.

Milo had to search for a rift on the wall to reach the man who'd spoken to him. The door had been covered in debris and rubble and there was no way that he could get in from that side. From the man's voice, Milo gathered that he was trapped inside and possibly badly injured.

Finally, he could see the man's greyed head, probably in his early fifties, and only two-three feet way from a pile of bloodied bodies. Milo could see that there were men, women, and children.

The trapped man had the back of his head, only inches away from the bodies and he seemed unaware of that. He had been near the door and it seemed that all that rubble that had caused the door frame to collapse had fallen upon him.

Milo struggling to keep down the contents of his stomach, without saying anything, started to remove the rubble from the man's body. The man had one of his arms free and tried to use it to help free all his body. It was almost dark when Milo removed the wooden doorframe and the man was entirely free.

'Give me a hand, I want to stand up if I can' he said almost in whisper, all the strength drained by his injuries and being under the weight of rubble for many hours.

Milo thought about the bodies that he'd tried to keep the back on them, scared to look at. Especially a young girls' look with big glassy eyes, made him feel guilty for what had been done upon them.

He felt like she was asking him to leave quickly.

She thought him as one of them. However, I do not feel as one of them and I cannot turn my back on someone that needs my help.

'I think you should not move, let me go and get help' Milo said hastily trying to convince the man not to turn and see the bodies. He felt that he could not cope on his own when that man would see all his family in a pile of bodies.

'I know what you're trying to do my lad, but do not worry as I know what is behind me. I dug them from the ruins of this house in hope that I'd find, at least one of them, alive and I all I found was their charred bodies…..' he broke and sobbed deeply for a few minutes.

'When this part of wall fell upon me I was trying to get out and bury them' he concluded between sobs. He managed to get himself in a sitting position. He had blood all over his body and Milo was not sure of how much injured he was.

'Who are you, are you from this village?' he asked suddenly and Milo shuddered at the answer that had to be provided.

'No I'm not from this village, but I am looking for… he almost said Vera's house,…. Besim Gashi's home' he corrected himself, realising that it would have been offensive to ask for a young girl's home in this village.

'You should go but I do not think that you'd find anyone. They've left early this morning for the mountains. If they reach them' he added as if speaking to himself. −You been sent to evacuate them, too late for that, far too late my lad. Go and see if you can find anyone to bury the bodies, which is the most useful thing you could do now. Besim's house is still standing and is just above ours,' - he explained exhausted trying to stand up. Milo supported him back on his feet. He was unstable for a few seconds than moved a little as if to help the blood flow and seemed that he had escaped with no serious, physical injuries. 'Tonight is too late to carry out any digging; we will wait for the daylight to come. It gives me some more time to be with them, and try and prepare them for burial. You go and sleep at Besimis' tonight. There is no way that you'd be able to catch up with them.'

Milo left without saying anything.

Once out, although dark by then, he still could make out the house contours, and a little cottage not too far from it. He swung the wooden gate open and rushed inside. The doors were unlocked and he checked every room, calling softly

'Vera! Vera!' He wasn't expecting to be answered.

He knew it was too late.

He ventured out, desperate to find some life signs. Within minutes he felt he was stepping on a mound of freshly dug earth. His body stiffened.

Pulled himself back and looked down. He could see a wrath and fresh flowers over which now he knew what it was. A loud sob escaped his lips.

'Oh my dear love was I far too late. Is that you under there?' he lamented going down on his knees. He felt like his heart was being ripped out and burst in uncontrollable, angry sobs. He buried his face in the soil as if to muffle his sobs and continued until he felt spent and his grief and anger simmered down a little.

When spent lifted his head, he felt that he had company.

Someone was standing behind him, quietly, holding a lantern or something to light the place with. Now he could see a photograph of a woman close to the wrath, which he could tell that it was Vera's mother. He'd seen her picture in Vera's little purse. Knowing that Vera would be in grief and shock, if she was alive, did not make him feel any better that the mother was laying in there and not her.

Slowly he stood up and turned around.
There was a woman and a young boy, who he gathered would be the woman's son.

'Where is she? The question escaped his lips without him realising that he'd used Serbian instead of Albanian as he would have wanted to.

'She left for the mountains' he heard the reply in Serbian while expecting Albanian.

That reeled him back to his senses, and started to introduce himself.

'We gathered who you are' he was cut off, midsentence by the woman's voice, 'but do come and spend the night with us.

–There is no way that you can find your way up to the mountains tonight,' she added in a warm and inviting voice which made him obey her cordially pulling hand.

'By the way, my name is Grada and this is my son Vasil. Gashi family is the closed we have to a family, or better we had,' she said notes of unspent grief and anger audible in her tone. The three of them went inside.

****

Vera was sneaking behind the building, when she heard something move behind her.

She stopped.

With her heart pounding stridently in her ears she turned, slowly, to investigate upon this new situation.

Within seconds, she realised that she had been silently hounded by one of the paramilitaries.

Like a trapped, wounded reindeer when knowing that the hunter is just behind and any effort to escape is futile, but still the life instinct makes it run for it, Vera sprang into a desperate attempt to elude whoever was behind.

Lucky for her that it was not pitch dark and she could, just barely see the walls of the buildings around to do a last second aversion and evade a hurtful bump.

She tried to remember the way that would lead her to the civilian crowd that she'd seen when she'd been hauled to the camp. In agony from the pain released from her leg and from fear at being caught and sent back, Vera felt all the strength drain out of her.

A few feet way she detected a thin strip of light resting on the wall of the building in front of her. She turned on her left, without turning to look back, and followed the narrow path trying to find the source of the light. It should be from the place where the civilian crowd is being guarded, she contemplated as she reminisced in her mind the corner she'd seen them last.

As she came running from behind the building out in the open well lit space, a last minute scan of the new situation brought her to an abrupt halt.

They were guarded, but luckily for her the paramilitary had his back on the crowd and leaning to the lamp post, smoked as in slow motion.

His body posture suggested that he was tired and sleepy. There were a good few feet between him and the sitting group.

Looking back if she was still being followed, she crept closer trying very hard not to attract guard's attention. When she was only two three feet way she was noticed by people in the civilian group.

There was a middle aged woman with an infant in her lap that noticed her first. She motioned Vera to move closer.

Once at her side the woman pulled her gently, as if she knew that Vera was wounded, to sit beside her.

Quickly, she took off her woolly warm cardigan and threw it over Vera's back, silently gesturing that she should put it on. Vera had had no time to think about the cold evening that had added to the misery of the fearful conditions that they were in. She was not feeling cold and she resisted taking the cardigan from the woman who, in her view, needed it far more than she herself. The look in the woman's eyes told her that she must obey.

'She will get us all in trouble' a male voice from the crowd whispered.

'Shut up Berat, as if we're not in trouble already' an old woman, sitting close to Vera whispered angrily back.

No one else said anything but she could see that many other

men and women shook their heads in agreement with the old woman, looking angrily at the young man. Just then she realised that he wasn't a lot older than herself.

As she slipped her arms through the still warm cardigan, Vera felt close to tears.

She had not thought that she could be any danger to them.

The old woman sitting on the other side of her was rummaging through her bag.

'Here, cover your head with this' she produced a head scarf. They won't be able to recognise you' she whispered.

Vera silently, touched deep in her heart, did as she was told. They were trying to protect her.

The very same thing that her mother would have been doing, protect her despite the dangers that the defence might entail.

The woman, who'd been the first one to notice Vera, passed her sleeping infant onto the lap of a man who'd been sitting on the other side of her and said nothing until then. As if reading her mind he said 'There is something to clean the wound with'. Without lowering her head to look she went through the bag, feeling with her hand. She found what she needed to clean the wound and the man holding the child, slowly and looking in the guard's direction, handed the woman a small pocket knife. At that moment the guard turned to look in their direction. Although there was no way that they could jump the electric fence, someone had tried and they all had seen him die, he still had to keep a close eye upon them.

The woman, preparing to clean her wound, stood still until she saw the guard's back again. Then she cut a big blood stained square from Vera's jeans, uncovering the gushing wound warning Vera that she'd feel a sting. She needed to make sure that no sound would escape her lips.

Vera assessing the difficult situation they all were in, shook her head firmly and looked determinately into the woman's eyes to make her trust her that she would be strong and keep quiet. The woman poured some spirit from a small bottle straight in the open gash.

The coldness of the liquid and the sharp sting made her body tremble, but no sound came out of her lips.

The cleaning seemed exceedingly long for the pain she was feeling.

She almost fainted.

Grinding her teeth she told herself that she needed to endure that pain if not for herself for these other people that had put themselves even in more danger by accepting her in their midst.

At long last the woman tied, quite firmly, in order to stop the bleed, one of her baby's sweaters around her thigh.

A few paces way a pregnant woman, Vera could notice her swollen big belly, tossed a cloth in her direction.

Unfolding it Vera could see that it was a long heavy fabric skirt and it was meant to cover her torn out jeans and conceal the dressed wound.

Stunned by the way that all these strangers acted, in silence, knowing exactly what to do for someone they had never seen before, she permitted herself to release her strong emotions through slowly descending hot tears that came from the very core of her soul.

Overwhelmed by day's events, tired to the bone, and feeling safe for the moment, she was falling asleep when she heard the old woman's voice again.

'The night is growing chillier, we need to get closer, as closer as we can and turn back to back to lean on each other. This should be done very slowly and quietly' she added whispering, but in a commanding tone.

Vera did not have to move.

Everyone around her shifted and she was surrounded by other people. Some of them had their back on her some faced her side. However they made sure that her wounded leg was kept straight and it was covered. The woman that had dressed her wound told her to lean on her back. They all huddled together as close as they could.

The warmth from the woman's back and the human kindness released in abundance from these people that she'd never met before, carried her gently into an exceedingly sweet dream.

She was following her mother who was watering in the wonderfully green field corns. The streams of water from the dam were going to the roots quenching their thirst and freshening Vera's feet. It seemed that it was one of the days when she'd come back from the city and having missed her mother for long months, she would not allow her out of her sight. The first few days Vera would follow her everywhere chatting ceaselessly, like two very loving sisters.

Then there was something and her mother wanted her to go and check the dam or something.

Then there she was falling into the dam which was filled to the brim with water. She wanted to call for help but she felt that she'd lost her voice.

No matter how much she tried to hold on to some stones that kept coming loose to her touch, she felt the earth sliding.... and she was going down.

At the last minute when she expected her body to hit the water she felt her mother's hand heave her up.

Silently, as she still could not release sounds, Vera was trying to thank her mother for saving her life, when she found herself hauled onto her feet by the woman that had dressed her wound.

They were enclosed by many more armed paramilitaries.

They had been told to stand and line up in front of the main building.

Through the shuffle Vera heard someone say that it was two in the morning. Standing she could notice that pregnant woman's acumen. The heavy fabric long skirt, slid down covering her bloody and dusty jeans. With the cardigan head scarf and the skirt she was not the young girl anymore. As long as she managed to keep her head down she was one of the plain looking women.

****

Pavle saw the girl melt with the civilian crowd.

'She might have a chance with them if I'm able to help her,' he considered as he went back to the doctor's room.

He was inspired by that young girl's bravery and he felt willing to risk more. He knew that the doctor was on his side; however it was very difficult to fully trust someone when the circumstances were dreadfully clear; you'd pay with your life.

Pavle came back and noticed that the doctor had made everything ready for the girl.

'Did she manage to escape?' the doctor asked casually. Seeing the obvious, she should have been back if she hadn't run off he added 'Good Lord, how brave, may God be with her! -Now our work here is done, we need to go back and tell them that she fainted as I dressed her wound and that she's lost too much blood. She needs some sleep to recover a little. I'll go and speak to Petar. He trusts me.' the doctor rolled up his equipment.

'Only God knows why he does when I hate him so much. I am sick and tired of what he and his dogs are doing. I am sick of the way he lied to me and got me involved in all this madness.

You may be asking yourself why I trust you?' he added after a long let out of what was boiling inside him for quite some time. Without waiting for Pavle to say anything he whispered;

'Because she did not escape my dear boy, she's still inside. There is no way that she'd gone past Dragan. He was watching the gate. You let her blend with the civilians. I know what goes on inside your head my lad. I know for the simple reason that what is in yours is very similar to what is sweltering in mine. When Dragan comes in here to fetch her for Petar, will find no girl. I'd be very pleased to see their ugly infuriated and disappointed faces. I heard that they are going to tell the civilians to cross the Albanian border if they want to live. Perhaps Petar is in one of his good moods.

Perhaps he is not in the right mood to kill. Hope that last until dawn. That is the time when the civilians will leave the building. I will try to delay their coming for her as long as possible. Until the civilians pass the gate. I hope to God that they do.'

Pavle went out and, from the faint light reflected from the main building, where the civilians were being kept; he caught sight of three paramilitaries gathering some tools.

He slowed down the pace.

He could see the slight glimmer of reflection, that new unused military shovels, waved in the air while on their way into the back of a pick-up truck.

Pavle did not dare approach these fallow souls.

They were chatting to each other as if what they were doing was the most normal routine of their everyday life.

He walked back, did not want them to know that they had a spectator, in faltering steps. He was about to be part of another civilian slaughter.

******

One, two three....... a paramilitary was counting them. Vera felt her blood run cold in her veins.
'This is the first time they're counting us' someone poked her on her back as if perceptive of that sudden stiffness released from her body.
'Walk on!'
One of the, obviously higher rank, paramilitaries growled at the frightened civilians. The pity of a line chained around the building. They were shattered from lack of sleep cold night and taut nerves of the high possibility of being killed. Heads bowed down, shoulder slumped and dragging their feet towards the unknown, they all were thinking, in different ways, but about the same thing:
Will they kill us, or let us go?
All the signs suggest..... they want all of us gone, Vera willed herself in thinking a little more positively. The moment that they all passed the main building's court yard and onto the unlit back of the building, they were ordered to stop. The child of the woman that dressed Vera's wound gave a sudden high pitch waling. His mother had her arms wrapped around him and was trying to comfort him by rocking him gently. Opening his eyes to the darkness and the order barked at them, seemingly had startled awake the infant.
'Shush that child!'
Someone from behind hissed irately. His mother was

desperately trying to nurse him, but to no avail. The situation was becoming heavier by the minute. Everyone knew that these hyenas were waiting for a slight reason to flip and start killing. *'As if they care for a reason, Vera thought to herself.'*
'Get in the truck, all of you!' the paramilitary that had just counted them howled, irritated conveying what everyone feared that they were at the brink of dropping the pretence of being humans. *'Being human includes tolerating children crying,'* - Vera spoke to herself again.
They started to push the civilians.
To avoid being pushed people started to move faster.
The crying child's father jumped in and turned to help his wife. Vera stretched her arms offering to hold the infant while his mother climbed in the truck. Vera felt the warmth released from the bundle that wrapped the baby in her arms and started to rock him gently.
Once in her arms his high pitch sounds slowly quietened down.
'You have a magic touch' her mother had said to her once when she'd tried to calm down her tiny thing of a brother. And she herself was only ten years old.
She could feel the child's body tremble as if from strong hiccups caused by the sobs that he released from time to time. The mother turned to help Vera while her husband motioned to Vera to hand him the child.
It was Vera's turn to climb in the truck.
 Once in his father's arms the child set off in, even higher than before, waling shrieks.

'Give him to her, it will be some cover for her as well' the woman said when Vera got beside them in the truck.

Rocking the infant became difficult as there were too many people boarding and there was not enough space.

Vera noticed that a whole company of paramilitaries were lining up.

They all had machine guns slung in their shoulders.

Her feet were hurting because they seemed to have connected with some sharp objects. She moved her left foot along the object, the right one was blocked by someone who had stepped on it, hoping that that metal object should be one of the drivers' tools.

Before she could make her mind up about the object that was hurting her, she heard someone lament 'They're going to kill us. I saw the tools that they've assembled to bury us.'

'Oh it's you again Berat, can you just shut up!' another male voice interjected angrily.

Fear leaped at her heart.

Although she knew from the outset that killing was on their cards Vera could not bring herself in accepting it.

It was madness.

Sick.

Absurd.

Nothing was making any sense.

Her brain started to get muddled up.

The thought of children getting killed elbowed all the other thoughts at the back of her mind. And she'd seen at least six including the infant that she was holding in her arms. Vera couldn't see, any of the children at that moment. Within minutes they were so tightly packed that if she had to fall she could not. The child was not making any sound at all. She could not tell if he was asleep.

'It seems you have a magic touch for children' his mother whispered. Same thing said in such entirely different circumstances.

Her already wounded heart received another chisel.

'I am not removing him from your arms until we're in the move. It may be hard for you to hold him, but he may start again' Vera was distracted back to the frightful situation they were in.

Vera did not have time to answer.

The engine started and very shortly after Vera felt a huge amount of weight on her back as she was squashed trying to hold back and not hurt the baby. Soon everyone regained balance and she was squashed again but the amount of pressure coerced by the weight was lifted.

'Pass him to me now' the woman said.

Vera let go of the child and as it was not possible to lower her arms down on her sides, she placed them on her chest. She still could touch the child with the back of her hands while her chin almost touched the nap of his neck. She could even smell the sweet scent, 'baby smell' as her granny used to say about her baby brother.

Not much of passing him to his mother, Vera thought, *I still can touch him.*

Luckily for them both he kept quiet.

Vera thought that some of the men would be able to jump off the moving truck and escape. She wished she'd been close to the edges. It was impossible to move and get closer to the edge.

It is out of the question to move my feet away from that metallic sharp object, let alone moving closer to the edges, she thought in desperation.

She was sure that sooner rather than later they were going to kill them. She had no time to completely contemplate what was going to happen to them, when the truck came to an abrupt stop. She heard the paramilitaries barking at them, ordering them to get down.

People were, stumbling on each other, as they were terrified that they may get shot at if they did not move fast enough. Vera, very soon, pushed forward by other people, felt her feet touching earth.

It was the crack of dawn, and the stars had started fading away. Vera could, just about figure out the sort of place they had stopped at.

It was a steep narrow valley. There were, sparsely scattered, some shadowy bushes. It was a quick scan to detect any possibility of escape, but very soon, her hopes died way.

They were surrounded by so many paramilitaries, that she thought that there were as many paramilitaries as there were civilians.

Women and children were ordered to separate themselves from men. They all started, listlessly, moving. It seemed a deliberate slow move as they all knew in their hearts that that was the last moment that they were seeing each other.

An old woman, just two feet on Vera's right, hugged a young man tightly for a few seconds and did not want to let go. Her son pushed her gently away.

'I can stay for you' -she was whispering desperately, tears streaking down her cheeks.

'No mother, it does not work like that –you need to go' he concluded trying hard to swallow his own tears and pushing her tenderly.

Vera turned her head on the other side. It was too much to bear. She felt her heart tremble and about to give way. Her throat was aching for the deep sadness she was feeling and the strain put on it to resist crying. On the other side her eyes met with a young couple's tight embrace. They hung on each other, crying quietly.

'They're newlywed' someone whispered.

The young woman had buried her face on her husband's chest with her arms tightly wrapped around his waist.

'Move fast or you get shot!'

A paramilitary howled at them.

The young man was trying to break free from his wife's arms. She would not let go.

'I want to stay with you!' she cried in a quiet but firm voice.

'No!! Let go!'

Her husband managed to free himself.

'Come on bitch, he is thinking of you' a paramilitary interposed cynically.

Then the young man, quietly, cupped her face in both his hands and spoke gently to her all the while looking into her desperately frightened eyes.

'You're young you need to live for both of us.'

Vera could no longer listen. She did not feel that she had tears to shed. She wanted to scream for all the pain she was feeling. The scream was stuck in her throat and felt like she was having one of those bad dreams when you want to scream your head off, but you're paralysed and can't. She walked way in a bid to be on the side that they were told to. She had no one to part with and yet she felt that her heart was bearing all the sadness that these mothers, wives, and sisters were feeling. She had never met any of them before, and still could feel a tremendous amount of pain, witnessing their heart-breaking parting.

By the time she reached the side where woman and children were gathering, dawn had settled in and she could clearly see the tears streaking down trying to wash away the deep sadness etched in their faces.

She could feel the fear.

She could feel the pain.

Just one look and one could touch their pain and fear for their loved ones.

A young boy no more than twelve years old was sobbing uncontrollably. His heartache wafted off his body in slow languid waves entering Vera's heart, causing even more pain. She wondered how much more she could hold. She felt like exploding with heart ache.

A child of about six, seemingly parted with his father, came, and hugged tight against Vera's wounded leg.

The agonising pain caused by the child's pressing down with

both his arms, sprinkled stars in front of her eyes and her head swam in a daze for a few seconds. She tried to, gently, unwrap his arms to no avail. Vera bent down, hardly bearing the pain, and asked him if he knew where his mother was.

He did not speak for a moment then pointed in the men's direction and said;

'*Baba* is there.'

'Okay let me hold you in my arms.'

It was the only possible way to make him release her wounded leg. She was very close to fainting with pain. He, finally, let go and raised his arms to get up. It seemed that his father had ordered him to go and join the other group and, apparently he had no one else from his family.

Vera might have resembled an older sister or someone close to him to cling onto in this harrowing experience for his young life. Although the child did not seem too heavy, she hesitated to hoist him up. She did not know if she had enough strength left to stand. She took hold of both his little hands and squatted down. Then reminded, from another strong bout of pain released from the wound, that it was an impossible position for her leg, she slowly placed both knees on the dewy grass.

Vera was about to ask him for his name, when she felt his small arms tight around her neck.

His little head came to rest upon her chest. Her chin touched the top of his head.

At that precise moment Vera heard a loud shriek.

The young woman that did not want to leave her husband was being pulled by two older women. She broke free and run back toward the group of men held to one side by the paramilitaries. Vera could see and understand the look in that young man's face.

Love and pain mingled to the point of being inseparable.

He knew for certain that they both would be killed.

Then she looked at the faces of the paramilitaries and froze. They were smiling at each other.

Their look foretold the drama that was to befall the young woman, sooner rather than later.

Vera had to stand and walk as the women and children's group was herded away by an armed group of paramilitaries. She pulled the child by his hand as she was sure that she had no strength left to hold him on her arms. Luckily, the child did not insist into being lifted up. It seems that he was feeling a little safer now. She could tell by the tight clasp of his little hand in hers.

Vera knew what it meant.

He'd been forcibly separated from the people that he loved and trusted and he could not afford being careless and get separated again.

He had to hold on to someone he trusted. And she did not know his reasons for deciding that she was that person.

Vera was walking at the very edge of the road when she heard one of the paramilitaries radio signal bounce off. He'd been walking right behind her. She did not get what was being said to him, but she heard him answer:

'Yes sir!' And in no time he yelled:

'Everyone stop!'

Vera's couldn't help thinking that it had something to do with her. She spotted one of the repulsed faces that she remembered from yesterday, going up close and glare at every woman's face. She then knew that she had no chance of escaping again. Surprisingly, she did not feel anything about herself, but she felt a dreadful new pain reach within every inch of her being.

It was the child.

He had to be forced, again, away from someone he felt safe with. The paramilitary was manhandling badly all the women he had to look at. He pulled their scarves down then pulling them harshly by their hair would turn their faces to face him. When realised that they weren't who he was looking for, he'd shove their head back with such force that Vera thought that twice she heard neck bones crack. And he'd do that with such contempt that one would say that when he saw their faces they were covered in dog crap.

Vera thought that she should not allow other women suffer on her behalf. She asked a woman close to her to look after the boy, who would not let go of her hand. He clasped tight both his hands over hers and pleaded:

'Please Vlora do not leave me again! Pleaseee!'

Only then she understood his hold onto her.

The disturbing events had played havoc with this child's mind. This Vlora he was trying to hold on to might even be dead. Similar to what had happened to her little brother Joni.

The terrible events had muted and made him very obedient. Only the thought of him and his unknown whereabouts sent cold currents through her heart. She'd promised both her parents to look after him. She tried this time more determinately to break free from boy's tight grasp and passed his little hand to the woman who thought that he was Vera's brother and could not come to understand why she was abandoning him.

'They are looking for me' Vera whispered to the woman. 'Other women are suffering because of me and there is no way that that pig will not recognise me.'

Just then it seemed that the woman recognised her as the young wounded girl that had come in their midst when they were in the camp.

'Hush he may not recognise you. Take that chance, he is not killing us, we can put up with that' she whispered pinching Vera hard in the back of her hand, as it seemed the only way to get through to her.

The other woman's reasoning and willingness to help stunned her. Although she was a complete stranger to her Vera thought that she had a point and she should listen to her.

A few more women and would be her turn to have her face glared at.

Her heart quickened its pace.

The little boy had gone all quiet after he'd retrieved Vera's hand. He was leaning on her for comfort. From a distance one would have thought that they were mother and son. Only close inspection would ascertain that they weren't even brother and sister. The little boy had a light shade of dark skin and curly jet black hair. Whilst she had a blonde's white skin complemented by her fair straight, shoulder length hair.

She even stopped breathing when she felt the paramilitary's' hand toss her headscarf on the floor and grab her hair hurting her. When he turned her to face him the boy gave out a loud shriek, distracting him into thinking that he was her little boy. *He's scared that I'd be taken away*; Vera thought and tried to break free from the paramilitaries' very brutal hold, to comfort the little boy.

For the moment he released the hold on her hair and made Vera believe that the little boy with his loud shrieks and yells had saved her life.

She hoisted him in her arms and buried her face in his chest, trying to comfort the boy and hide her face at the same time. Just when she thought that she was out of danger, she felt the air stiffen around her. All the women had guessed by then that they were looking for her.

The deeper the quiet before the storm, the stronger the storm would be, her granddad's words echoed in her ears.

And the tempest is coming for me she thought, but still refused to turn her head. She could picture the paramilitaries', sudden stop, and turned to look towards her again. It was the moment when she felt the tranquillity of the treacherous storm to come.

He was back and this time he grabbed her even more violently than before and was breathing in her face.

He let go and moved a little away as if to gather momentum and hit her so hard on her shoulder that the child was shaken off her arms. His rifle butt was about to be used again when he was distracted again by the child's loud shrieks.

Then he changed direction aiming for the child.

Vera realising that he'd kill the child if the rifle butt caught up with child's top of the head, threw herself over his little body. Vera took another excruciating blow on her back. The women next to her pulled the child out of the way.

'I found her!' He hollered to his comrades. And dragging her from her hair he started his way back to the point where they had gathered all the men. There were most of their forces, surrounding the civilians.

Before she reached the point where they'd been made to climb down of the truck she was shoved aggressively down. She could see that she'd landed very close to the army boots of someone of higher rank. Then with no time to take in some mouthfuls of air to feed her lungs, she was kicked up on her feet to face the paramilitary the shiny boots of which she'd encountered while on the floor. She stood gingerly and being very worried for the traumatised little boy, turned to look on the women's direction.

The torn crowd of women and children slid slowly out of her sight.

She did not hear the child scream as one of the women had taken charge of him, comforting him. Poor little thing, as long as someone was holding his little hand he would not make a sound. He seemed to assume that any woman was Vlora, whoever she is and wherever she may be, Vera thought.

Vera turned to face the angry paramilitary who somehow seemed amused and entertained by this girl's guts to annoy him. No one had dared and no one would ever dare he thought. It was the same face that had ordered for her wound to be tended to.

With no time to gather her wits, the shiny boot slapped her hard across the face. It seemed that he'd felt humiliated by this young girl's defiance.

'Take her aside and make sure that she sees everything that is going to happen here!' -he ordered the scarred face that started grinning in Vera's face. It seemed that he'd been looking forward to such order.

He pulled her aside and forced her head up.

Her head tended to hung down from the lack of sleep, tiredness and hungriness.

Vera had forgotten about eating, the bullet wound and the fresh blows that she'd received had all added to the already distraught body and brain.

Then she looked at the crowd and was petrified to discover that the young boy, who she'd seen cry hiding behind his mother, was among them. And so was his mother. Although he'd ceased crying, he still seemed very frightened and they, he and his mother had their arms tightly wrapped around one another's waists. The woman's look was one of defiance.

'I know you are going to kill my little baby you barbarian shkies, but I am not giving you the satisfaction of bending and crying in front of you.'

Vera thought that his mother had possibly seen other deaths in the family. Her thoughts about the woman and her young son were interrupted by another wail.

The young couple were forced brutally apart.

He was being held down from three paramilitaries while his wife was being dragged a few feet way. To Vera's immense horror they pinned her down and started to tear off her clothes. Her husband realising what was happening lurched forward to only be met by a strong blow at the back of his head from one of the paramilitaries. He resisted the blow and refused to stop trying to break free. He kicked the paramilitary that was blocking his way and was very close to breaking free when one of the paramilitary raised his gun and hit him with the barrel hard close to his right ear. Vera saw his knees buckle and fold slowly as he crumpled on the ground. He stretched both arms in his wife's direction and soon stopped moving.

His wife fighting her own battle, trying desperately to fend them off, had not seen what had happened to her husband. They had to knock her unconscious to make her body yield to their demands.

Vera shut her eyes in futile attempt to keep her memory clean from such a sickening view. Just before she forced her eyes shut she noticed that the whole crowd as if commanded by an invisible hand turned their backs slowly. It seemed as if they wanted to prevent such view from assaulting their eyes in those last few moments their earthly existence.

The shiny boot paramilitary bellowed some kind of reprimand to the scarred face. Vera felt the results of that yell on her hair. It was so ferociously pulled that she thought that he was scalping her. The pain was immense but she still refused to open her eyes. She did not know how long he could keep pulling her hair. If she tried to release herself she knew that he'd pull harder something that she could not afford. Her scalp was burning like hot tarmac was being poured into it. She endured all the pain for a long time. To her it felt like hours had passed since he'd grabbed her hair.

Suddenly he released his tight grip on the hair. She did not want to open her eyes terrified of what her stare might be met with. But the total silence that had ensued suggested that something even more sinister and barbaric was about to transpire.

She decided to open her eyes.

The air was charged with strong currents of fear.

It seemed that everyone was holding their breaths in collective horror.

Vera looked at the crowd.

Like in a slow motion movie she observed the young man's face. He had spoken so tenderly to his mother earlier.

She could read it all over his face.

Pure human fear tinged with anger for having to die so young. Then she looked at the child and she thought that if she was able to get closer she could touch his fear.

Looked at his mother and she seemed prepared to die.

Watched the man who'd been struck down when he tried to protect his wife from being raped. He'd come around, but barely could stand. It seemed that to him it no longer mattered if he died or lived.

He had already died.

Vera looked all those faces that she'd never seen before but felt as if she had known them all her life for all the pain she was feeling. She could see the paramilitaries with their guns aiming at the crowd and waiting for an order.

Vera was finding it hard to breathe.
She saw the shiny boot man move his hand.
The fire erupted from all directions straight into the crowd.
The bullets rained from all directions.
Some fell down instantly, like harvest crops, some started to run only to be caught by bullets a few feet away from the crowd.
Terrified screams were chiselling Vera's heart.
She looked at the child's face, his body had been covered by his mother's body toppled onto him, and his eyes told her that there was no fear anymore.
There was agonising pain.
The pain of dying. She saw how his eyes flickered and the face slowly change colour. The whiteness of death spread all over his face.

Vera felt her head swim in daze. She thought that all her insides were being ripped out by a giant viper. She remembered her grandmother saying to her; '*Look after your little brother even when he's asleep, because vipers love to find a baby sleeping with his mouth open so they can slide in and get hold of his heart and lungs.*' She'd been terrified and had stopped playing with children outside and sit close to her little brother's cradle, when he was asleep. Once her mother had found her looking over him and asked her why was she doing that? She had laughed at Vera's explanation and said to Vera that her grandmother had tried to scare her into making sure that her grandson would be properly looked after. Although her mother had tried to explain to her that a viper coming into the house to do that was extremely unlikely, she had not managed to shake off all the imagined ghastly feeling in Vera's head, if that incurred. It was exactly what had ensued those moments that Vera was convinced that it was not her imagination, it was materializing.

She could see the viper's body and long tail wagging on the ground while it tried to get hold of her heart and lungs. The moment she saw the body of the young boy falling to the ground and his mother toppling over him, she thought the viper had finally got to her heart, ripped it off, and was moving backwards, to come out. She felt her body turning into a hollow, empty hose and her head felt woozy as everything became dark again.

She could see her mother again beckon her to come to the field corns and help her with watering. When she came around discovered that she was in a bed, but somehow could not move. She thought that she was in a dream again, but the stench of strong male sweat snatched that thought quickly away. To convince herself that she was not dreaming she tried moving her hands, only to discover that they were firmly bound to the beds' iron bars. Tried moving her legs, and although could not see them, she could tell that they were rigidly tied to the bed as well. Some frail morning rays of sun had penetrated the window glass and were resting on a slanting position over Vera's stomach.

She heard voices nearing the room she was in.

 Vera closed her eyes.

Vera contemplated who would be going in.

 She did not want to see when the 'shiny boot' man came in.

 It struck her that she had found a name for him and that she just knew that this was his room. He came in and slammed the door shut, hurting Vera's ears.

Soon after, she could gather, he was stripping off his clothes. The pong became unbearably stronger. She had not experienced that if the stomach was empty as hers was now, the repugnant smell would make her want to throw up. She could tell that he was over her because he'd blocked the rays of sun that had warmed a little patch on her belly.

He was breathing over her face.

Although she continued to keep her eyes shut, his disgusting breath, garlic, and strong spirit, laced with the strong whiff of sweat, forced her into a violent process of being sick.

She had nothing in her stomach, and only some yellow water came out of her mouth, but forced her to open her eyes nonetheless.

The first thing that she took in was his vest, the only thing he was wearing. It was so filthy that she thought it had been months since it had seen any wash. And it was in such big contrast with his immaculately groomed face and hair and the army suit with shiny boots, which he had on when executing the civilians.

Without saying anything, and quite unexpected he slapped her hard across the face. She looked him straight in the eye with defiance and contempt. She could see that he derived great amount of pleasure from hurting her. He pulled harshly at her top and when he did not manage to rip it off of her he turned his back and was looking for something. In seconds he resumed work using a very sharp, pocket knife, to cut her clothes off. It seemed that he did not want to take any chances and release Vera's hands or legs. He'd noticed the fighting spirit within her. He did not care, in fact to Vera seemed deliberate, that he was drawing blood by cutting her skin quite deep at places, while cutting off her clothes.

When he harshly pulled her jeans down, as far down as the bounding would allow, Vera was only thinking of one thing; how to throw him into a rage so he beats her senseless. When his face was close to hers, taking bits of her top off, she spat vehemently straight into his eyes. She had gathered enough saliva to almost blind him for a few seconds. That was bound to fling him into a rage.

He stopped.

Slipped out of the bed and went at a corner, next to the door, of the room.

She heard the tap running and him splashing his face with water. When he turned she was sure that she did not need the next mouthful that she had made ready, just in case.

His face was red with rage and jumping on the bed he kneeled beside her with his fists ready for a violent beat.

Within seconds she was out.

Her already battered head, from the harrowing experience, did not need much boxing over to black out.

******

Pavle was deliberately walking past in the corridor where

Petar's room resided.

He'd gone in only a few minutes after Petar had entered the room.

Walking swiftly as if passing, he'd listened for any sound that would come through the thin walls but he'd heard nothing.

He wondered if she was alive.

He could not shake off the feeling of guilt.

He'd asked that question to himself for the umpteenth time:

Why does her life matter when I have witnessed so many civilian killings?

And he'd come up with the same answer over and over again; although not intentionally he and his friend had played a great part in what was happening to her.

Suddenly some repeated thumping caused him to throw caution to the wind and stop close to the door.

The sound released when a strong fist connected violently with someone's scull, allowed no room for being mistaken.

Still there was no sound that could be figured out as released from the girl's mouth.

Pavle thought that she was dead and Petar feeling cheated by her death was venting his anger over her corpse.

He went out and met the doctor and Dejan smoking a cigarette near the front gate.

Once they caught sight of him they turned and motioned to him to join them.

'You should not beat up yourself about what happens to that girl, son –the doctor directed Pavle. There is nothing you or anyone can do, as it's directed all from above. The masters are holding the strings while we are living the nightmare of their sordid play.'

He offered Pavle a cigarette and Dejan lit it for him.

At least he could relax a little in their company.

Not long after that they spotted Petar coming out of the building. He'd put his army suit and boots on, but had not done all the metal buckles. One could easily spot his filthy vest underneath that glossy shine of army clothes.

He came near them and without saying anything snatched Pavle's fag from his fingers.

Pavle froze.

But when he saw him pull into the cigarette and then hand it over to him again, he relaxed a little.

Ignoring the doctor he motioned for Dejan and Pavle to follow. Just a few steps away from the doctor he stopped, turned to face them and said:

'Take her to the river. Kill her and push her body into the water. Make sure she is dead before you toss her body down. If it turns out that she's alive you'll be killed and thrown into water. Is that clear?'

'Yes sir!'

They both were aware of what would ensue to them if the girl turned up alive somewhere, anywhere.

Then he turned and went to the doctor seemingly to have a fag with him.

When they went inside the girl was still unconscious.

Her body uncovered dreadfully assaulted and abused.

They both, as if thinking the same thing, went to cover her body.

'How are we to walk her to the river if she cannot stand?' Dejan asked. Pavle untied her hands, inspecting her bruised and swollen wrists. The same had happened to her ankles.

Near the sink, Pavle spotted a jug. He went and filled it with water, while Dejan was trying to gently pull her jeans up and do the belt.

Pavle came and sprinkled some water over her face.

She did not stir.

Then he squirted some more and paused to observe the difference in her face.

Her eyelids twitched twice.

He spilled a little more and she finally opened her eyes allowing a feeble moan escape her bloodied lips.

'We need to be quick; he said more to himself than the girl and his friend. They are having their breakfast now and if we manage to go unnoticed we may be able to do something.'

She looked at them and did not give the slightest hint that she remembered who they were.

From her expressionless eyes Pavle gathered that she'd lost the will to live.

They got her standing on the bed and could see that her top could not be assembled to cover her body anymore. Swiftly he took off his short sleeved shirt which he wore underneath and pushed it gently down her head and holding her arms through the seams he whispered to her:

'You have to cooperate with us to save your life,' and expecting no answer he gathered her top around so his shirt would not be recognised when they walked out.

They had to pretend that they were being harsh with her otherwise Petar would suspect them and sent other paramilitaries to finish the job.

They walked out.

Dejan first, pulling the girl from her ragged clothes, while Pavle brought up the rear with his rifle poking the girls back.

Petar turned to look at them and was not even remotely bothered for any close inspection. He turned to speak to the doctor again, while the doctor gazed at them over Petars' shoulder and discretely winked at them.

Pavle knew what he meant; that he'd delay Petar as long as he possibly could to make it easier for them to save the girl.

When nearing the main gate, they stopped and Pavle walked back.

He asked permission from Petar to take one of the truckers to finish the job more quickly.

He said that they could.

Pavle went in and using the key which he found in the front seat, tried to turn the engine on.

It gave a spluttering sound and went dead again.

After a second attempt he managed to send the engine roaring and it seemed to have drawn the attention of those that were inside, having breakfast.

He rushed to have the girl and Dejan at the back of the truck and leave before they came out.

He knew that if Dragan came out it was the end for the girl and maybe for them too. Dragan had his doubts for them quite some time back and if he started to plant them on Petar as well, they'd be in great danger. They had to get out quick and at the same time pretend nonchalance.

He drove towards the main gate and came to a slow halt waiting for the paramilitary in charge to open it for them.

Pavle was looking at the paramilitary, who seemed to have all the time in the world, and wanted to kick him into moving faster.

To make it look like he had some kind of power, not just manhandling the main gate, in his hands, to boast his status a little, he came closer desperately slowly, to Pavle felt like hours had passed, and was about to ask something.

Pavle kept inspecting the courtyard through the side mirrors.

If they did not get out in less than three minutes they were in great danger.

He noticed that Petar was motioning to the gatekeeper to let them pass and at the same time he observed that Dragan and the scarred face, he'd never tried to learn his name, came out rushing.

As they were approaching Petar and the doctor, Pavle was weaved out by the gatekeeper.

He did not even look in the mirrors but accelerating harshly was out on the road.

He flung a quick stare back to see if they were being chased by another trucker and seeing that it had not happened just yet, gave him more hope.

******

Vera was staring vacantly at the road they were passing on. It was the same road that they had taken early in the morning. She noticed that the grass at the roadside was covered in the morning dew. Although the sun had come up not much warm was being released by his yellow rays.

The clouds gathering from south forecasted a rainy day. They obscured the sun which tried to send down some rays through any thin rift managed by the wind.

She could see small patches of sunrays scudding over the grass trying to suck up the morning dew.

She had forgotten where she was and did not want to be reminded.

She used to chase the morning sun rays when she was little.

Trailing the sun rays where she could her eyes came upon a big heap of freshly dug earth.

Immediately she was back in the reality.

They had not bothered with digging a big hole and bury all the civilians. Instead they had shovelled around and covered the bodies with earth.

It struck her that the main reason for choosing the steep narrow valley it was its muddy soil, easy to shovel.

She felt nothing, only numbness, perhaps she was drained and hurting and weak to feel anything.

The truck was crawling up a steep uphill when she noticed that they were being followed by another truck from a distance.

She did not bother to work out where they were going to stop and kill her.

She knew and she felt as if she welcomed it now.

The face sitting next to her seemed vaguely familiar. She did not want to bother herself with trying to figure it out either.

Why should she?

Only a few minutes left of my life.

They reached the peek, the place where they had violently snatched her from the crowd, and started downhill. There was another valley they were coming into.

She tried to retrace the sun rays in a bid to move away from the tormenting reality.

She did not find rays anymore and thought that the sun was completely draped by the dense clouds which promised torrential rain.

Suddenly she felt a deep shudder infiltrate her traumatised mind and battered body. Her eyes had come to rest upon another heap of freshly dug earth.

She was surprised for she was feeling sharp stabs of fresh pain entering her heart.

She thought her heart had died that morning.

It seemed that it was still there and was aching for the women and children that were led to believe that they were going to be spared killing. They had done that only to have two smaller mass graves instead of a big one.

Unexpectedly the truck came to a shuddering jolt.

The driver came out and offered her some biscuits saying that she was going to need some strength in her. It was not much he said but there was nothing else that he could get for her.

'Get it down you it will help with what you're going to have to go through.' And he was explaining quickly, how they were being followed and how they were going to pretend to shoot her and she should pretend that she had been shot and fall down. And the hard bit he'd said was that they had no choice but to push her into the river and had paused and asked if she could swim.

She'd said nothing.

Of course she could swim.

But she did not want to swim.

She wanted to die.

He'd said that he had no time to spare as they wanted to escape with their lives for themselves. He told her that they were going to run way but if they suspected that she had not been killed they would be on their backs, and there would be no way for them to run way from all that madness. They needed her collaboration he'd concluded leaving the small packet of biscuits in her lap and walked swiftly back in and drove off.

The paramilitary accompanying her at the back spoke for the first time saying that his friend was right and that she needed some strength and there was not much time to spare. She paid no heed to what he was saying. Her mind seemed to register very little of what was transpiring around her. The road came close to the river and kept going along sneaking through valleys and around the feet of a succession of hillocks.

At last the car stopped.

They walked her to the very edge of the river, holding her by her arms.

'Pretend as I instructed you! This is the only chance that you are going to get. We can't see them but they are watching us!'

With that they moved swiftly back leaving her barely standing. A few feet way they raised their guns. The machine gun shots pierced the damp morning air, severely hurting Vera's ears.

When they did not stop shooting, Vera remembered that she was supposed to fall down.

Just to save her ears from hurting she decided that she should fall. She was not sure if she'd heard him right. She was not sure of anything now.

The next thing she felt was her body plunging into the river. In the few seconds that followed, just before her head hit the water, she saw her mother's face appear on the surface.

She was frowning at her.

As her body immersed into the icy cold water, sending shivering arrows within every inch of her, she stumbled back into her senses.

Her immediate thought was Joni and his whereabouts.

That was enough power to fuel her into a feeble flap of swim to save her. She came to the surface and dimly saw the two paramilitary's silhouettes. She went under again and resurfaced a few paces down to feed her lungs with air. Looked up and saw nothing. She let the current take her downstream. By then she had assembled her wits but sadly she noticed that there was not much strength left in her. She had to use it wisely or she would drown. It did not take long for her to figure that out.

Her life was hanging by an extremely emaciated thread. Although she'd come to her senses, she had to fight the cold and the strong currents with an awfully weak body.

Suddenly she felt that her back had connected with something solid and was held by it. She could make out that it was an uprooted tree trunk fallen into the river. Slowly, supported by the branches she managed to hoist her body over it. She thought that she could have a little breather in there.

Very soon she discovered that she wouldn't be able to as the tree under her weight started to shift downstream.

She decided that she would stay on it for as long as she could. She did not know for how long she stayed on it but she had a feeling that the current was pulling her under.

Vera noticed that she was approaching a huge vortex. In seconds she discovered that she was going to be sucked under. She prepared herself as much as she could by drawing in and holding quick deep breaths.

She went under and thought that was it.

It was the end.

She was going to drown as the pull was very strong and there was no way that she could swim her way out.

******

Pavle and Dejan walked swiftly back to the truck and drove off. They were driving along the river bank and Pavle kept flinging over the river fleeting glances, scanning the surface for a body rolled over downstream by the current.

But his stares were met with angry currents frothing as if a giant viper was wagging its huge tail in it.

When they thought that they were too far for Petar's *dogs* to catch up with them, they relaxed a little.

Dejan rummaged through his backpack and fished out some ham and small slices of white bread.

'Did not know that you had food in you, why didn't you share some with the girl?' Pavle was feeling anger swell up in him and feared that he'd lash out in the only real friend that he had.

'She did not eat your biscuits; if she'd tried I would have given her more. *Their* inhuman ways are not contagious, luckily,' Dejan concluded with a ghost of a smile playing over his lips as he wasn't finding funny his attempt to enlighten their mood a little.

Pavle understood.

He pulled over and accepted the food and with his stare sliding languidly over the river surface he started to eat.

'There is someone coming toward us!'-Dejan said alerted.

Pavle turned to see a young man gliding downwards and coming to a halt a few feet away from the military truck.

He seemed to hesitate coming any closer.

Pavle got out and walked slowly, trying to work out who that young man was.

Was he Albanian or another armed Serbian paramilitary?

If it turned out to be the latter, they'd be in grave danger as they'd be seen as the *'great cause'* deserters. As he went closer he was met with very familiar face features, but for some reason he could not contemplate, Pavle found he was lost for a name.

He wondered if he'd gone wacky.

The look on the other man's face told him that he'd been recognised too. However, somehow the other man seemed hesitant to say anything and was waiting for Pavle to break the ice.

'Milo! Is that you?'

Finally it came to him.

And without waiting for an answer he extended his arms to embrace his dear old friend. Milo did not move nor show any sign of being happy for bumping into his old friend.

'Come on it's me, Pavle!'

He still was trying to convince him to return the surprise that they'd met in such a place and very unusual circumstances.

The look in his old friend's eyes told him to keep the distance. Pavle lowered his arms and noticed that Milo's eyes were inspecting his faded shade of green of his army uniform.

Then he understood and started to explain slowly and disgracefully the reason for being in the army uniform.

At the end he said hastily that they had deserted and were fleeing.

He warned Milo of the camp forces and all the killings that they'd witnessed.

Milo brought out a photograph of a young girl and asked if they'd seen her.

The young girl's tender and loving look at the person behind the camera and her beautiful smile was the greatest shock yet for the day. They both realised that the happy girl looking at them from the picture was drowning in the river. They, without even looking at each other intuitively knew what to say to Milo.

'No old friend, no we have not seen her, and you should listen to us and come with us. If you go down there they would force you into joining them.'

Milo told them how he'd spent the night with Vera's neighbours and how the young man had offered to lend him his bicycle. Then, with eyes down, they told him how the paramilitary had killed a civilian crowd; men women and children. Their description of the civilian crowd matched that given from Grada, Vera's neighbour, about the crowd that Vera had left the village with. Their last account, although he was spared the details of the gruelling execution, hit Milo very hard. However, he could not come to accept that Vera was dead. He'd go with them for a few miles and when far enough from the camp he'd get out and continue his search.

'There is nothing you can do or say to change my mind' he'd concluded leaving no scope for discussions.

They knew far more than they'd said but sensing his love and determination they said nothing more, apart from goodbyes and advice to take great care as it was an extremely dangerous area.

Milo took a footpath with his bicycle which was more of a hindrance than help now that he left the road.

The first drops of rain left their marks on the dusty road. The winds seemed to pick up and very soon sheets of rain obscured everything around. Pavle could no longer detect anything from the river as the road was moving gradually way from the river bank. *The chances of her surviving are painfully slim;* he thought and did not want to share it with Dejan as he could see that his friend's thoughts mirrored his own. It was written in his eyes and the way that he looked at the river. They concentrated on their way out and back to their home in Serbia. Nothing was going to stop them now that they were behind the wheel.

******

Vera heard voices around her and tried hard to open her eyes. The eyelids seemed to have been laden with some cold heavy metal for all the weight and chilliness she was feeling.
Soon she drifted into darkness again.
Natalia and her seventeen year old daughter had been herding their cattle down the river to drink water. It was the first day they had come out after all hell had broken loose in their village. All houses around were burned down to the ground. Finally, the rain had managed to fully extinguish the fire.
Natalia hoped that with the fade way of the curling smoke absconding from the heaps of rubble that had draped the sun for days, would fade away the acrid smell of burned bodies. She had come to this village a few years back. Soon, after the previous president dying, many people in Serbia were promised work and land in Kosovo. Her husband had registered with the army, while she had found work as a nurse in the city. Very soon she had discovered that Albanian nurses and doctors were being fired and replaced by Serbians, perhaps just like her, made to think that there were vacant work positions. She had worked

for some time but soon after her daughter was born she'd decided to stay home and raise stock. Her husband's wages were quite good and she'd supplement with the stock.

She had found the neighbours, hostile at first, but soon after deciding to stay home, they warmed up at her. Although they had accepted Natalia with her daughter, they'd never had accepted her husband. Her closest friends would leave her house as soon as he was through the door.

She had tried to build a bridge but it seemed that it had remained all frail and would crumple down easily at any time. It seemed that her husband had contributed to it by appearing arrogant and hostile in his army uniform.

When confronted by Natalia for the ways he behaved toward the Albanian in the village he'd replied nonchalantly; 'I want them to know who the boss around here is.'

She had tried to reason with him, saying that nobody would like a boss in their own home, but she'd been dismissed for he had loads of paper work to catch up with. He'd gone into his workroom and had required that his supper should be delivered there. With that, she'd gathered that he did not like her being too friendly with the neighbours. He had changed so much lately. She had started to notice that they were growing apart.

First cracks of their married life had appeared soon after he'd gone out for a drink with her brother in law. She had wondered if her brother in law, her sister's husband, had his finger on the way her husband perceived and behaved with Albanian neighbours. She had known for quite some time that they, brother in law and his mob, including her husband, were preparing to fight. But she would never have thought that the fight was going to be directed upon women and children.

When Natalia went in, her best friends' and closest neighbour ruins of the house, found her clutching at her two dead children. She was writhing with pain herself and later dying in Natalia's arms. Natalia had asked her daughter to come and help to bury them.

From that day, this was the first day to come out as the cattle had to have water or it would die too.

When she came across Vera's body washed aside by strong currents, Natalia thought that it was a corpse.

The strong will to help that comes with being a nurse, sprang into life. Although it had years of sleeping inside her, she still knew how to check for a pulse and provide the necessary first initial steps to bring the unconscious around. She asked her daughter to bring the mule about and both of them hoisted Vera on its back. It had no saddle on and Natalia instructed her daughter how to gather and herd the cattle back home. She, herself had to go ahead and help the girl who may be suffering from hypothermia. The girl nodded, gazing sadly in Vera's face.

******

Vera could hear voices. She thought that she was sleeping at her parent's home. A wisp of delicious smell, floating from something being cooked tickled her nostrils. It drifted down worming its way through her empty intestines. From the power that the smell had to stir the hungriness in her, made her think that she seemed to have not been in touch with food for quite some time. But, somehow she did not find the smell familiar.

'Mum, mum she's waking up' Vera heard a female voice calling out. Vera felt puzzled. Why, the person close to where she lay was speaking in Serbian? She felt as if she needed her hands to lift her eyelids. As she tried to lift her right hand, a searing pain ripped through her right shoulder blade, and decided against it. Could not lift her arms. Tried again to open her eyes, and.... succeeded. She noticed a young girl, perhaps a little younger than herself, smiling warmly at her. Another woman entered the room and Vera gathered that she was the mother. It was an older version of the female that was standing close to her. When the older woman spoke, Vera immediately thought of Grada, their neighbour. It was the same accent in her Albanian, only smoother and more fluent. 'You're in safe hands now. Just try to have some rest' and she swiftly, walked out of the room again.

Vera tried to speak but found that her tongue was swollen and that was an impossible, at least for a while for any sound at all to come out of her mouth. She closed her eyes again, ignoring the girl's smile. She felt terribly weak and tired. Any little move that she tried to make would coerce an immense amount of pain upon her body. So she decided to keep still and gather her thoughts.

In slow motion it started to dawn on her. All the terrible events that had transpired that morning swam in her view, stabbing gushing wounds in her heart.

The little boy's terror-struck eyes and the young man's face as death stretched its steely fingers upon, flashed back the bullets that rained over the civilian crowd. The way they all started to fall like, harvested crop under farmer's sickle, made her heart bleed. She felt deep down sobs, like hiccups, something she'd never experienced before.

However, she could not contemplate how she came under the care of these two women. She heard feet shuffling, just outside the room she was in. She was surprised at her strong sense of hearing. She could even hear the girl's quiet breathing. Vera tried hard to command her brain into forgetting the events of that morning. It needed to focus on the new situation she found herself in.

She opened her eyes again and saw the woman with a wooden tray in her hands, nearing her bed. The smell of food brought strong bouts of hunger which hurt her belly. The woman placed the tray on the side and with one hand parted her lips gently while with the other she spilled some warm soup into her mouth. Vera felt devoid of any emotion. She did not try to eat the food but she did not refuse it either. It seemed that survival instincts were winning over the dying will that she remembered having lately.

Her tongue burned and stung like hell, her throat ached. It felt like every molecule in her body was hurt somehow.

She could see that the spoon was small, like the ones they used to spoon feed Joni when he was little. But she still thought that it loaded her mouth with too much food. She turned red as she tried to swallow.

The woman, sensing Vera's discomfort, filled the spoon with very little soup. It was a slow and painful process, but Vera could read the woman's pleased face as the food was almost finished.

The woman, finished feeding, and told her that she should try to get some more sleep.

Obediently, Vera closed her eyes but soon she found that she could not sleep. Thoughts about what had happened and Joni's whereabouts refused to vacate her brain. Both women had left the room.

Suddenly, she felt she needed their company, human company.
Girl's quiet presence had warmed her heart. Now that she was gone Vera felt that she'd liked the girl being there. It served her tired brain as a reminder of humans still inhabiting the earth.
Slowly turned her head and looked at the only window.
The rainy, pitch dark night had swallowed all the surroundings. It had stopped raining and it was very quiet, too quiet. Vera wondered if this house was somewhere up in the mountains, for all the tranquillity around.
Soon the poor state of her body succumbed into a fitful sleep.

******

After a long, wet and very cold trek, Milo spotted a faint light. The dusk had settled and was becoming harder to follow the path. As he drew closer the light grew a little stronger. Milo

hoped that it was a house where he could shelter for the night.
It was a house and the light was emanated from an old lantern placed on one of the two windows of the house. It looked directly onto the path, the end of which brought Milo in the doorstep of a two storey house.

He slowed down and stopped. Milo, clumsily, clambered down. His legs ached from the long peddling. He walked and stood in front of the window. Milo squinted at the window glass. Apart for his faint reflection, he saw nothing. There was no way of telling if anyone was inside. A wave of apprehensiveness washed over him. He wondered if it was fear of what he might find. '*What* if there were the Serbian paramilitaries and asked me to join them?' Milo terribly dreaded.

'What if they are Albanians and want to retaliate?'

And for the question that he daren't ask himself: 'What if there are only bodies?' He did not have time to conjure up more questions. He heard feet shuffling inside.

The door opened slowly and an old woman emerged at the doorstep. 'Nik is that you?' she asked.

It was dark and quiet and the old woman's strong voice shook Milo into an answer.

'No...' He said slowly and was thinking what to say next when the old women reiterated:

'Nik! Niko my son is that you?'

This time the voice was even stronger and it struck Milo that she may be partially deaf.

'No! I am not Nik!' He almost shouted back.

'Oh are you a friend of his then? Do come in son do come in. I am sorry these flaming eyes and ears play me up. There is nobody else in the house. My only son has gone to the city to get some supplies and has not come back.

I am getting worried about him.

Those cursed cars that run through the city do scare me. If you're not careful then they may get you.'

The old women led the way while talking, supporting herself on the walls, tracing her way back in.

Milo followed.

Once inside, Milo took in the surroundings.

The dim, flickering light released from the lantern placed on the window sill, revealed a small coffee table close to the fireplace. Two worn out sofas stood on both sides of the fireplace.

Slow burning embers made him aware of how cold, tired and hungry he was.

He sat and extended his hands over the blazing embers. Slowly he started to feel the warmth steal in. 'What did you say your name was?' She asked while opening a shelf next to the door.

Suddenly he struggled for an answer.

'Milo, my name is Milo' he had to repeat in loud voice after a few seconds of hesitation.

He felt all the air stiffen around the woman.

She held her breath for a few seconds then slowly put down a bowel she had got grasp of. And started towards the table, sure of her footing.

'You have not come to tell me that something bad has happened to my Nik, have you?' She demanded in a tone which suggested that she desperately hoped that that was not the case.

'No! No!' Milo was quick to answer this time.

'Then what brought you all the way up here? There should be something. I am deaf and cannot see well, but I do not think that I have completely lost my marbles.'

'I ... Milo started reluctantly. I was on my way to visit my auntie that lives quite far from here. But my bike broke down and I had to walk. Then the storm and the rain slowed me down.'

Now that he'd gotten used to the dim light, he could read her face expressions. It told him that she had not bought his story. His slight accent would have been another hint...... He knew that she had gathered that he was Serbian.

He pulled his hands away from the fire and interlacing his fingers, he placed them on his lap. Prepared himself to listen how his nationality would affect the way that he'd been treated from the second he set foot inside, up to this moment.

'You must be hungry and tired son. I will try and put something warm in front of you. I don't know what happened to that daughter of mine or my young granddaughter. It is not like them to not come and look after me for this long, especially when Nik is not at home.'

When Milo remained silent and did not feed her conversation she stumbled back on her feet and went at the farthest corner of the room. Just then, Milo noticed a cooker and wondered if she had been able to cook anything.

There, as far as he was aware had been a power cut for more than three days. It took her a while preparing something. She returned holding a wooden tray in her hands. The smell of a mixture of leeks, cabbages and meat wafted from the tray, stroking his nostrils.

It made his mouth water.

It reminded him of his grandma and the leek and cheese pies that she used to cook.

'I tried to keep it warm for Nik. The power's cut off again this evening. Who on earth is playing with the electricity?' she carried on not expecting any answer while placing the tray on the small coffee table. She pushed it slowly in front of him.

'Tuck in, I hope you'll like the leek pie and the lamb and cabbage soup. I still got some saved for Nik. He should come tonight.'

She's had days with no one to talk to, Milo thought about old woman's way of talking. She kept speaking out loud and not expecting answers. It was like she was conversing with herself.

He took a mouthful of leek pie and thought that he had not tasted anything better for quite some time, not since his last holiday with his grandparents.

'Umm...it is delicious' he managed to say while wolfing down everything in front of him. The old woman sat down with a satisfied smile playing all over her face. After a while she stood up and quietly, went into the next room.

She reappeared, holding a bundle of clothes in one hand and a lit torch in the other.

'These are Nik's clothes, from your shadow I can tell that you're the same build and they'll fit you. When you're finished, if the electricity returns, you can have a shower. If not I think you should change into Nik's pyjamas and go to sleep. I'll show you the room' she concluded and placed the neatly folded clothes, next to him on the sofa.

She went and sat on the other sofa and almost at once a fat tabby cat appeared. It leaped onto the sofa as well. Very soon it curled up sleepily, resting its head half on the old woman's lap and half onto its fat belly.

'Oh good you're back! I wondered if you'd deserted me as well' she said softly stroking the cat's head.

'I know Nik would never abandon me,- she carried on as if talking to herself, -but I am a bit angry with him for taking this long.'

Milo finished eating and slowly, stood up to put the tray way. He did not know if the woman would approve of him clearing away.

'Thank you!' he blurted at last and hesitantly walked at the corner where another table stood. It was bigger than the one he had dined on.

An electrical oven sat on it.

Somehow, he felt guilty.

Is her son going to, ever come back? He, acutely, doubted it.

'I didn't buy the story of your auntie, what is your real reason for coming all the way up here young man?' -her voice, although soft, it had some sharp notes which cut harshly through his grave thoughts nonetheless. 'My real reason.....' he stammered and then suddenly decided to tell her the truth. 'My real reason is that I have fallen in love with a girl from the village on the other side of the river. I heard that something terrible has befallen her family and......I came to see her' the last part was hastily stated. It was as if he wanted to assure himself that he'd see her again.

A deep within smile crept over her lips softening the edges of the weathered and creased face. Milo's last words seemed to have wakened some profound and very delicate feeling that lay beneath that rough, hardened by life's unfair tricks, face.

'I have loved and I run away with a young man from a catholic family. I turned my back on my family, who did not accept him. I left the city, and came to live the hard life of the mountains. I have not regretted, not a single minute, although I was very young when I took that decision. Whatever it is that has befallen her family, the love for each other will help to heal. And I suggest you come and see where you're going to sleep. It seems that you have a long journey ahead of you. Tomorrow night you must reach your sweetheart's home.'

With that she stood up swiftly, as if some of her old and sweet memories had taken away long years of hard life. Grabbed the torch and motioned to Milo to follow her.

Milo trailed her footsteps wordlessly up a short flight of stairs.

****

'They're coming, they're coming' the girl's cries woke Vera with a jolt. Shshsh... Who's coming?' Her mother asked her in hushed tones. Between girl's sobs she could just about make out *army* and *dad.* She wondered if the girl's dad had been involved in what she'd witnessed the day before.

Vera looked at the window.

A faint light was penetrating the satin curtains. She could tell that it was very early in the morning. She summoned all her strength and managed to get up.

The situation became clear to her.

She had to leave as soon as possible.

What if the shiny boot man was with them and found that she was still alive? She felt pleased that she could walk, just about. The wound in her thigh bit hard whenever she touched the ground with her left foot. It didn't matter, she could walk. Whilst her right shoulder blade felt a bit better than it had when she'd fallen asleep. Last night, while asleep, she reckoned that she'd heard voices. More voices, more people, besides the the woman and her daughter. But she couldn't be sure.

She scanned the room for her clothes. She could not detect any of her belongings in there.

Vera noticed that she was wearing a thin, pink night dress. She thought of opening the door but felt too weak. She had to go back and sit on the bed. The girl burst in and Vera could easily see that she'd been crying, although she tried to hide it. The girl noticed that Vera was wake and sitting upright on the bed. She approached the bed and stood in front of Vera. She hung her head while trying to say something. It seemed that she was too upset and words could not become audible. Only a muddled jumble came out and she started to cry.

Vera felt she had to comfort her.
She understood her difficult position.
She extended her arms turning her palms upwards and the girl slowly, placed her hands in both with a tight grip. The girl bend down on her knees she placed her head gently, on Vera's lap.
Vera stood up gradually, pulling the young girl with her. Without saying anything they found themselves embracing each other like long lost friends.
The door opened and the woman came in with a bundle of clothes in her hand. Almost immediately, Vera recognised the bundle as her belongings. She let out a long sigh at the scene in front of her.
'Two young girls that had never seen each other before were united by the common fear of senseless deaths surrounding them. They should not have a care in the world apart that of trying to look good and attract boys' she thought while throwing the bundle on the bed and joining in their hug.
Vera felt weak again and releasing herself from the group hug she sat on the bed. 'I know what is happening and I should leave as soon as possible' she reiterated something that she'd told herself only a few moments before. Vera looked at her clean clothes and waited for them to leave the room, so she could get dressed. They apprehended the look and left the room silently. She was feeling shaky but she knew that they'd be in great danger if an Albanian girl was found with them.
She did not know how and if she had any strength left to reach the mountains. All she knew was… that she had to try.
When fully dressed she left the room supporting herself by the

walls. She could hear more than two people speaking while nearing, what it seemed a large living room.

As soon as she was in their view, they all became silent. There was the woman that had looked after Vera with her young daughter. Also, there was another woman in her forties and a boy of about ten years old.

The girl and the boy stood up to make space for her on the sofa.

'This is the woman that has kept in touch with us since this terrible thing started' - the host woman stated without bothering to introduce them properly. Time, or the lack of it, had not granted permission for long introductions.

'Her other son has been forced to join them. But at least, he is keeping us informed. By midday today they'll be here. But we decided that I have to be home and wait for my *beloved* husband, when he comes with his *pack* -sarcasm and contempt visible in that sentence, especially, *'beloved husband'* phrase. - She and her son go with you. The mule will carry you. She knows where to hide you, at least for now.' The end came a bit abrupt as if unsure of what more to say.

The other woman and the boy made for the door. Vera tried to follow. 'No, no you sit here -the woman pointed at a chair close to the door, while I harness and bring the mule.'

Vera sat slowly.

Every inch of her body was sore. It hurt followed by any move that she tried to make, no matter how little.

Vera heard hooves in the courtyard and prepared herself to get out. She tried to haul herself up in vain.

She could not.

All three women rounded her and helped her, as gently as they could, to mount the mule.

'I will bring the mule back as soon as it's safe' the other woman spoke for the first time and it was in Serbian.

Vera noticed the girl's frowning look towards the woman and she knew the reason. Then hurriedly the girl went inside reappearing a minute later with a bag. 'Here are some clothes and some food' she said in a low voice.

'There are some tablets as well, try to take them' her mother added in the same low voice, as if they were embarrassed of something.

'I'll pray for you' the host woman said motioning to the boy to pull the mule out of the courtyard. In minutes they were out of the ironed gate and in the street.

The boy was in front pulling the mule, his mother following silently behind. It was another day with rain on the way.

It was morning, but it looked as if dusk was settling for all the dark, heavy with gathered rain, clouds. They hadn't travelled for longer than twenty minutes, when a tremendous bang shook the earth.

Vera thought that she'd heard the whooshing sound above their heads, only a split second before the bang.

The boy turned to look at her and his mother.

Although trying not to show it, Vera could see in eyes the amount of fear that he was feeling inside.

They had neared the river and were walking alongside it. It seemed that the army was shelling one of the villages at the foot of the mountain. And that was the mountain they intended to take cover in.

Vera spotted the old flimsy bridge that they all had crossed two days before. Very soon, she realised that the woman wanted to take her at the same cave that all the survivors from her village had gone into. Or…the one, she hoped that they had reached….

'I want you to return, I can reach the mountain on my own. I don't even know why you helping....' another loud bang cut her off.

She pulled the harness from the boy's hand and said; 'I'll find a way to return the mule' and with that coaxed the mule to go on.

A few paces away she turned to look at them. They were still there, not sure whether to turn back with the mission not completed, but their lives no longer in danger, or carry on.

A third bang even louder than the previous one seemed to have tipped the scale of hesitation as they sprang in a frantic run.

Vera was pleased that they were going back.

She coaxed the mule even harder. All she wanted now was to reach the mountain. She recognised the path that they all had followed after crossing the old bridge.

It seemed so very long ago, what with all what had happened. It all sounded as an indescribable nightmare. There was still some part of her who believed that she was having a bad dream.

She reached the mountain. She was scared to turn and look. She just carried on through the path.

She had to hug tightly to the animals back in order to escape the pine branches with her eyes intact. The path was very narrow and almost closed up by branches intertwined in each other by opposite sides. When she reached some undergrowth she despaired. The path pronged. There were two different directions.

She had no idea which one to follow.

She pulled the harness to signal for the animal to stop. It did and almost immediately, took to grazing at the side of the path. She thought of dismounting it, but decided not to as she had a better view from up there. And she did not know if she could climb back on it all by herself. As she tried to open the bag and find something to eat, her eyes caught a piece of clothing. Even though covered in blood somehow that piece of clothing seemed familiar.

She climbed down landing harshly. In haste to get to that piece of fabric, she forgot all about her wounds. Her heart was almost turning over with the rapid speed of beating. She started to limp towards that piece of clothing. She had, finally, gathered that it was from her mother's dress.

She remembered how she'd shredded it and dressed Fatmir's wound. There was no path anymore but it was all undergrowth. And she could see that there were even more signs that some unspeakable event had taken place.

Vera had no heart to follow but she knew that she had to.

The trail led to a slopping hill at the end of which lay the bed of a dried torrent.

With great difficulty, Vera slouched down and started to assemble with a trembling heart and hand her mother's dress fragments.

Bending down, close to a shrub to get another piece, this time a larger

one, her eyes met with a bare turned blue, foot.
Slowly, she got up and looked a little further down when she discovered Fatmir's whole body.
Head downwards, face, with open eyes, staring at the sky, one leg under the bushes while one entangled over the shrub he'd fallen over.
She did not stop. She had to find her brother.
Vera half rolled half dragged herself down as she reached a clearing.

What came into her view almost immediately reminded her of a similar scene.
Long ago, when she was about eight years old, she'd followed her grandfather, without his knowledge, to search for a flock of lost sheep. They'd found them butchered by wolves.
Almost half of their entire stock had been slaughtered. She had been terrified by the blood and the sheep's slit throats with scattered and chewed on body parts.
She'd become ill and not eaten for days after that encounter.
She reeled back to reality.
The way that their bodies had fallen on the ground suggested that they had been ambushed. She recognised almost all the faces that she'd seen that day.
All fallen at different angles. Where someone's feet lay, rested someone else's head. There was no sign of Joni, or the young girl that had trusted to look after him. Vera could see the young girl's pregnant sister. She was among the dead.
Did they take the other path? Vera did not stop to think for too

long. Her heart had hardened. She'd changed within two days from a person who could not stand the sight of a tiny drop of blood, into a person who trampled through massacred bodies. She thought herself as one of them, dead body, sooner or later.

Only Joni mattered. He should not be one of them. He was too young and she'd promised to look after him. Vera closed her eyes tightly to shut out the sickening view of dead bodies.

Stood like that for a few minutes than slowly opened her eyes.

A few feet away she could see the ghost of her grandfather. Right next to him it was the image of her, at a young age.

He was stroking her hair. Then suddenly stopped and looked in her real direction. He spoke as he used to when she was little.

'You can't control the boat on the ocean of life my pet. It may meet a thunderstorm that destroys everything. But you can control the decisions after that. And not giving in when you hit rock bottom is the most important of them all!' and slowly evaporated in the air.

That was all she needed to hear at that moment. Vera knew that her desperate brain had conjured the image of her grandfather. And the words he said were words of wisdom she'd heard from him among many more. But not giving in was one she needed to hear at that very precise moment.

She had to get back where she left the mule grazing.

Ascending was a struggle as the wound shot searing bouts of pain with each move. She decided to trail the other path in hope of finding her brother, '*alive*' she whispered to herself.

When she managed to get back to where she'd left the mule, she sat down wincing with pain released from the wounded thigh.

After a while she thought that she'd gathered sufficient strength to mount the animal. She staggered back on her feet and slowly drew near the peacefully grazing mule. After two painful attempts she managed to haul herself and only just, get hold of the rein.
She coaxed the animal feebly and started towards the other path. She was in search of anyone who'd managed to escape with their life.
 The trail led her into descent. Very shortly she saw a crystal clear small stream leisurely flowing down.
 As soon as the trail delved into the stream, the animal stopped and started drinking.
Vera did not disturb it.
Then the trail took a right turn and began pulling upwards. She was deep in the forest when she heard voices.
First she thought that her shattered body and mind were playing tricks on her. But the further she went the stronger it grew. She heard a child's cries and an angry woman's voice. Then unexpectedly it all went quiet. As she drew closer to the voices, she thought that she could see the source, she lost them completely.
She ordered the horse to stop by pulling the rein.
She tried to listen intently.
Vera noticed that she'd forgotten to breathe while listening to the *wind* she said to herself in despair. She did not want to accept that all she'd heard had been in her head.
Then on the verge of giving up on those noises that she'd heard and waddle on, she decided to call her brothers' name.

'Joniiiiiiiiiii!' she cried,
'Joniiiiii'
The pine trees echoed the name back to her.

Although she was able to distinguish her call and the fading echo she still liked to tell herself that there were people in there. And all she should do was shout even louder.

She called again and listened.

But all she could hear was the light wind whispering through the branches. She was about to resume following of the trail she'd been on, when she heard a voice calling out to her.

She thought she recognised Azemi's voice and hear heart leapt into her mouth. Vera became oblivious to the first drops of a cold rain that fell on her face. The drops blended with all the sweat that anguish and despair had extracted from her body.

She held her breath hoping that she'd be able to identify which direction the distant voice was coming.

She didn't need to hold it for long.

The second time her name was called it was nearer and it was clear to her that she had not been mistaken.

'Stay where you are, I saw you and I'm coming to get you' Azemi shouted out to her to make himself heard.

In a few minutes Azemi appeared in the clearing. Vera stumbled down the horse and tried to run toward him only to find that she did not have any strength left.

Her wounded leg had gone completely numb and she swayed, nearly falling. Azemi rushed to her side and she leaned on his shoulder.

She managed to ask 'Is Joni alive?

'Alive and well' came the reply.
All she wanted to know. She let herself go.
All the fear and emotion coupled with the physical pain had taken their toll.
She vaguely felt her body being mounted on the horse again and voices. Among all the voices, there was a familiar one whispering her name. She knew it was Joni's.
When she came to she found herself in bed.
She scanned the room to figure out where she was and spotted Joni's head. He was sleeping in the bed next to hers. Within minutes she heard a voice 'She is wake!'
A young man came in her view with a clipboard and a pen in his hand. 'Hello there!' he greeted happily. Where are we? Vera asked. She was perplexed by the fact that she could not figure it out.
'You are safe. You are in a camp and about to board a plane to Germany' came the short succinct explanation.
'But…how….where is this camp?' she wanted to know more.
'You have been out for more than 24 hours. When you reached the camp we put you on the drip and cleaned your wound. It is healing well.
And you will be ready to join your uncle in Germany.'
Two other men came in and woke Joni. They opened a stretcher for her.
She tried to stand but the doctor pushed her back gently. The two men lifted her into the stretcher.
Only then she understood what was happening. She had no will or strength to question that decision. It seemed that her uncle

had been looking for them.

Once out en route for the plane she looked around in efforts to spot any of the familiar faces. Her heart lifted a little when she spotted the girl she had trusted Joni with. Vera smiled at her and she smiled back.

She lifted her hand to be united with that of her brothers'.

He clutched it tightly reminding Vera of the unfortunate boy, who had clung to her during the harrowing events of that dreadful day. They boarded the plane. She looked outside of the window and felt her heart contract. She'd had no time to think about Milo. Now she was thinking that she may never see him again.

Her brain reversed to the first day when they'd met. Vera had been deeply absorbed in her studies when she'd felt a warm presence take a seat next to hers in the quiet small library. Slowly, she'd turned her head and her eyes had met his. They both had smiled in unison as if they'd known each other. He'd whispered shyly that there had not been another vacant seat in the library. Vera could not muster another look at his face, found him very handsome.

There had been quite a few sittings together at the library before he could pluck the courage to ask her out. They both had, as they had revealed later, sought each other's company. She remembered their first date. They'd had coffee and had walked and sat by the river bank. The spring sunrays had warmed their backs as they sat gazing at each other's eyes. They had beheld each other's gaze for a long time. She had been unable to speak. For the first time she'd felt something deep within stirring. Vera had thought that he had just walked out of Sappo verses 'He is more than a hero' and was sitting right next to her. For the first time she had been trying to define love. Later in her diary she had written: *What is love like I wonder? Is it like the soft drop of the summer rain quenching the earth's thirst? Or is it like the wings of the butterfly creating a small rainbow above the flowers it flutters around and stands on? Could it be like the running of a lamb towards its mother? Or is it like the sweet scent that floats in the air originating from a beautiful rose? Maybe it is like the strong pull of the two opposites of magnets. Is it like the strings of 'qiftelia'* that vibrate in unison to play the music of life? Maybe....all I know is that it has opened my eyes to all the things that I had not noticed before. Perhaps at the very core of life's meaning stands love. Maybe it's just the light that enters your soul...and turns the silent of night and moments of solitude into a celestial melody that only those who love can hear.* While the plane took off soaring in the sky like an eagle escaping from its captors, Vera's heart lamented for her dead mother and friends. It mourned for the young boy that had hugged her tightly. Her heart bled for the young woman stretching her arms towards her beloved when life was forsaking her. It grieved for the young boy that let out the last breath under his mother's lifeless body. She lamented for her country once blessed with life and now flooded in blood and tears. Her heart wept for her soul leaving behind all what she knew. A last question hovered in her lips: *Will I see him again*?

****

After a long treacherous journey Milo reached the mountains. He neared the cave following the directions issued by the old woman. He had managed to avert the paramilitaries and their camps and made it to the mountains. Milo heard feet shuffling just behind him and turned to investigate the noise. Before he could make out the source of the noise, something hit him hard at the back of his head. Milo fell hitting the ground hard. Everything lurched into a deep darkness.

When he came around found himself sitting upright, leaning against the trunk of an oak tree.

Before opening his eyes, he smelled the trace of a cigarette. Slowly, blurred at first the features of a man's face floated in his view. Right in front of him, a young man of no more than 17, was poised on a severed tree trunk.

Milo observed that his own hands were tied behind his back. The young man had his riffle standing next to the tree trunk he was sitting on. Milo gathered that he was Albanian as he was wearing civilian clothes.

'Where am I and why have I been tied up?' Milo queried in Albanian. 'Because you are a Serb!' a curt reply came from the young man guarding him.

'Do you know where is Besim Gashi and his family?' asked Milo again ignoring the hostile look delivered by the person in front of him.

'Oh, asking for information now are we?' came the sarcastic reply. 'How did you know that I was Serbian?'

The man did not answer just pointed at his wallet in the front pocket of Milo's jacket. His driving license had been there.

'You still got everything in your wallet…just wanted to know who you were…,' said the young man standing in front of Milo.

'Look, I'm looking for Besim's daughter, she is my fiancé?' he ignored the wallet business. He didn't care even if everything had been stolen. It wasn't important to him right now. He lied for the last bit, 'fiancé' in vain efforts of convincing his captor.

'She's been sent to the camp; nearly eight hours walk from here. The camp is in Kukes, Albania. And I hear she's going to Germany' he added reluctantly, as if not sure if he should share that information.

'Let me go pleaseeee! I need to see her!' he asked pleadingly. Milo thought that if he'd be on his way now, might be able to make it to Kukes before dusk.

'No I can't, I have orders' and turned around and called 'Axha Azem, ky serbi asht qute!' in Albanian –uncle Azem the Serb is wake!'

Within minutes two other people appeared in front of them. 'He says that he is engaged to Besim Gashi's daughter' the young man explained to the two new comers.

'What!' A howling shriek escaped from the lips of the one called Azem.

'He is lying. Vera is not engaged to anyone. I'm going to kill him,' he cocked the rifle pointing on Milo's chest.

'Hold it!' the other, older man, commanded.

'I can tell that this young man has no part in any killing, just looking for his fiancé. We can't kill innocent people and turn into *them*!' he insisted trying to convince the one called Azem. He seemed hell bent in killing the young man in front of them. Milo froze.

The other man walked in front of the one that had the rifle pointing on Milo's chest.

He pushed the riffle up and indicated to the young man, who now was standing a few paces way with a very frightened look, to release Milo. The young man rushed at Milo's side, untied his hands.

He kicked him into standing up.

'Run!' he hissed in hushed tones.

The one called Azem was struggling to point at Milo.

Milo did not wait to be asked twice. He started running all the while expecting a hot bullet to discover its way through his body.

Run, run without looking back.... He could still hear their angry arguing voices.

It had been his lucky day.

He reached the top of the hill and disappeared.

He knew that he was safe for now.

Milo stopped to breathe, felt he'd been holding the breath waiting for the gunshot.

Within minutes he resumed running not only to extend the distance from his captors, but most importantly to reach Vera in time. Finally, he reached a point where he could see the camp from a great distance. Instead of slowing down, now that he could see the camp, he quickened his pace.

'*I want to find her before she leaves for Germany*' he was

thinking through his laboured breathing. He knew that he'd lose her if the plane got there before him. As if hearing his thoughts a roaring drone vibrated through the air.

Milo's heart took a stab as he saw the plane ascending in the sky.

He kept walking, half running and walking in places when he needed some air in his lungs.

He had to hope that Vera had not boarded that plane.

Tiredness, muddiness, hungriness all swept aside when he reached the gate of the camp.

'I'm looking for Vera Gashi' he informed one of the men guarding the gate.

'Vera who?' asked the guard while taking out a bundle of papers that seemed to be lists with names of people.

'Gashi, Vera Gashi' he repeated still working on his breath while waiting for the man to check for the name.

He followed list after list pointing with his grubby finger, stopped perplexed and asked again.

'Are you family?'

'Yes, I am' Milo answered without elaborating. He could see that the guard was not interested in the answer. His head was bent down over the papers.

'I found it!....oh no… you missed her. She left for Germany two hours ago. Time and date is added next to her name.'

Please, look it may be another Vera' Milo added desperately hoping that he was right.

'What is her father's name?' asked the guard.

'His name is Besim Gashi' replied Milo quickly; he could

hardly wait to see Vera.
'I'm sorry; the person you are looking for has left the camp.' The guard shook his head being certain that the person in question had left the cam. Milo felt weak at the knees. He bent down to avoid the humiliation of falling in front of a stranger.

****

Eighteen months later, Milo was standing at Munich International Airport. A small piece of paper in his hand. An address in it. He hailed a taxi and read the address to the driver. About an hour later he was standing in front of a building about to press the shiny button on the side.
Milo felt that he needed to take two for his breathing to come to normal. He pressed the button and waited with baited breath. The receiver was lifted and a female voice, sent blazing arrows to his heart. He thought that he recognised it. He heard 'Hello! Who is it?'
 Milo was not sure of how to answer. Instead he asked in Albanian 'Can you let me in please?'
'Who are you?' came a swift reply.
'Wait for me outside please' she added after hesitating for a decision.
A short while later she appeared at the door.

The look on her face was of surprise and perplexed at the same time.

Milo noted the changes in her.

Somehow she looked a lot older than her age. He approached to hug her, but she pulled back.

'Things have changed.... a lot' she started slowly, in a barely audible voice.

First thing that Milo's brain engaged on was that she might have found someone else.

'And no, I don't have anyone else, in case you are thinking that, but things have changed in a very big way' she concluded hastily. Her voice higher than at the beginning, resembling the boiling water that starts quietly and when full force boiling, blows the lid off.

'If it is to do with the war, you know I had no part in it and absolutely despised it. It is disgusting and inhumane what has been done on your people. But you know that it's not my fault....' Milo was interrupted mid-sentence.

'Come inside we'll talk more about it.'

Once inside he was greeted by a young boy who stood up on Milo's entering.

He said 'Hello' in German.

A few feet from where the boy had been sitting was a little baby, sleeping in its cot. 'This is Jon, my brother, -Vera introduced them, -and this is Milo a friend of mine,' she directed her brother. Milo looked around for the baby's mother. When he saw no one else, '*maybe Vera is looking after it,*' he decided and sat on the sofa.

'And the baby, is my little daughter, her name is Roberta, short Berta. I decided to give her that name because the first part 'rob' means captured, slave, in Albanian. And she is a slave to her fate being the product of hate and not love.'

Milo's face became the mirror that reflected complete and utter shock. Now *'things have changed in a big way'* made sense to him.

He was lost for words.

'Oh I see your reaction on your speechless face, same as that of many men that had their wives raped by those inhuman monsters. Many of them have decided to cut them loose as if it was their wives' fault. If that is what you think, there is nothing more to talk between us. I'll see you out' Vera concluded and turned to look at the sleeping baby.

'I want to believe in what my grandfather used to say, that a child takes a lot more from its mother and only a small fraction from the father. I think I will learn to love her as I could not wring her neck the day she was born. I heard that many young, raped, girls and women have wrung the babies' necks the minute they were born. People carry out actions that are out of character when under extreme circumstances. And God help me that thought has entered my mind more than once....' she stood and stared at the window.

Milo started slowly: 'I will not lie.... I never expected this. Many other thoughts of you, finding somebody else have plagued my brain, while trying nonstop to obtain a student visa for Germany.

Every day that passed I saw another mile added to the distance of reaching you. I could hardly wait for my visa, I thought of following the illegal route. My love for you is so deep that this is not going to stop me from asking you to marry me.'

He went near her and asked 'Will you marry me? If you have to learn to love your child than so have I, we will do this together.'

****

Four years later Vera had, finally, said 'Yes!' to Milo's marriage proposal. They together, rented a small flat in Pristina. Vera had managed to get back to her studies and entered university. Milo had been there for her every step of the way. Joni was attending college and little Berta had started nursery.

One early morning their home phone rang.

Vera rushed to pick it up as she always worried about early calls. She had never found her father or a grave where she could lay flowers. In her heart she always expected a phone call informing her about her father's remains. She had been told that her father had been captured by the Serbs when recovering from a chest wound in one of the villages near where the fighters were based. They believed that he had been taken to a prison in Serbia. Vera had gone there, and helped by Milo, had managed to check their prisoner lists.

His name was not there.

He was lost like thousand others that mothers, wives, sons and daughters were looking for. Now she expected his remains to be discovered in a mass grave as some were being dug up. After a moment of hesitation she picked up the phone.

'Milo!' called the voice on the other side that Vera recognised as her mother's in- law.

'Good morning! It's me Vera' she answered warmly.

'I'm a bit rushed, sorry Vera I need to speak to Milo urgently' she replied brushing aside the pleasantries of small talk.

Vera had warmed to her mother in law, although Senka was always quiet and even when she was spending time with them. She moved around like a shadow. One could hardly notice her presence.

She had never seen or heard from Milo's father. Milo had explained that he had fallen out with his father. For a long time, they were in no speaking terms. He never liked to talk about it and Vera had seen it as a sensitive subject and left it alone.

She went and shook Milo wake.

'Phone for you, is your mother' Vera handed the phone.

'You okay mum?' asked Milo.

Then for a few minutes he said nothing just listened to his mother's voice. 'I don't think I care that much mum, if I come it will be because of you not him. I will call you if I decide to come, but I doubt it' he ended the call. Milo explained to Vera that his father was dying and had asked to see Milo for the last time. Vera suggested that he should go. 'Only if you go with me' he added and stood to get dressed. 'I think I should come, although I have sensed that he never accepted me. Since he is on his last breaths I should go.' So, she decided, they both could go and see him. They arranged for Joni to stay with a cousin and decided to take Berta with them. Senka had never mentioned anything about Berta. Vera had thought that Milo had told her. And Senka being the kind of person that did not interfere in anybody's business had just gone with it. She adored the little girl.

That afternoon they arrived at the old family house, where Milo grew up.

Vera was a bit apprehensive.

She was going in a house she'd never set foot in before, and going to meet her father in-law for the first and last time, apparently.

Milo sensing her anxiety took her hand and stroked it.

The warmth released from his hand, reassured her.

She started to relax.

In his other hand was Berta's little hand who also seemed daunted at going somewhere she was unfamiliar with.

They, all three of them stood in front of the big iron gate and Milo pushed the button of the old rusty buzzer.

Within minutes Senka appeared.

She hastily pushed the gate and threw herself in her son's arms. She whispered 'At last.... he's got only a few hours left' sighting with relief.

Then she hugged Vera and squatted down to hug and kiss Berta.

'I should warn you, his face is unrecognisable.

He is a mess.

Cancer has eaten away at his flesh for years now.'

They all went in.

The sick old man appeared asleep.

Despite the cleanliness of the place, there was a strong smell of rotting flesh with a twang of medicine. It made Vera wrinkle her nose.

'Milo…. is here' Senka spoke slowly near the sick man's ear. His eyes flickered and after a second attempt he opened them. Milo was still standing between Vera and little Berta, holding their hands.

'I'm here father and with me are my wife Vera and my little daughter, Berta.' Vera's heart warmed, it was the first time that Milo acknowledged Berta as his daughter. *Despite her birth certificate that states 'unknown' next to the father line, Milo is her father now*' Vera thought to herself.

The sick, old man looked at them and signs of recognition were registered from his eyes. His face was a messy bundle of rotting flesh and bondages. Only his eyes were clear to see as nose, eyebrows and ears everything was mashed up. Senka was fussing with little Berta while bringing in some chairs. Milo was trying to converse with his father while Vera sat quietly and looked around.

Berta went with Senka.

After a few minutes her eyes rested on a picture erected on the small table next to the sick man. Vera did a double take and stood up. Suddenly all her body was trembling.

She neared the table and picked the frame. The eyes of the 'shiny boots' were looking from the frame, straight into her troubled soul. Her fingers got numbed and the glassy frame was dropped on the tiled floor. It got shattered in thousand pieces. The noise made Milo turn and saw the back of Vera fleeing outside. Within minutes he followed her and stood by her side, very puzzled. She was throwing up violently and moved way from Milo.

'Vera what is it?' he asked perplexed that could not help.

'It's him!' she shouted pointing toward the house.

'He is Berta's father!' she added through uncontrollable sobs.

Milo looked for a place to sit as his legs could not hold him anymore. Senka had been a few steps away when Vera hurled the last sentence which was like stones thrown by children on the back of a dying stray cat. 'And the ghost of that black cat is me, and always has been, since I bore a child with the sick bastard' Senka thought audibly.

They both, Vera and Milo turned and looked at her.

Milo picked Berta up and pulled Vera gently.

'Good bye mother! Hope he doesn't die, not for a while. He needs to suffer a lot more than he already has. I will not come to his funeral.' Senka looked at them, tears filled her eyes. As soon as they were in the car Milo said: 'This was the past, now we're leaving it behind. A new life waits for us' and drove hastily to reach their home where, despite the smallness of the flat, love flowed in abundance.

Vera wondered; *'How is it possible that such extreme cruelty and unlimited love, both dwell in the human soul?'*

****

Press reports about Kosovo in 1999

Sunday Times *reports of 99 graves found in **Kastranic**, southern Kosovo. Surviving villagers hid in the surrounding hills for several weeks. They told KFOR the killings were committed on 9 April 1999 by Serb paramilitaries.* (Press Reports)

13 Jun ***Independent on Sunday*** *reports ethnic cleansing by Serb paramilitaries supported by Army artillery in villages near **Podvujevo**. Also of a massacre witnessed by an Albanian women of 6 men and 1 women (she also knew of 10 other dead and rumours of others) that was carried out by Serb paramilitaries in **Pishino Selo**. Eye witnees reports (both Serb Army and refugees) Press Reports*

15 June 1999: ***The Mirror*** *reports a "makeshift graveyard" containing 65 bodies in **Koleic**, 5 from one family. The murders were carried out on 19 Apr 1999 by Serb paramilitaries. The village itself has been destroyed. (Press Report) 15 Jun 1999* ***The Independent*** *reports the hamlets of Stagova, Rumjev and Kotlina are almost entirely destroyed and depopulated.* ***The Daily Star*** *reports that 27 people aged between 15 and 62 were killed by beatings and with grenades in **Kotlina**. Press report*

Goden and Zylfaj *-20 teachers killed on 25 Mar 99   Press Report16 Jun 1999* ***The Mirror*** *reports a refugee convoy of some **250 people massacred** at **Meja** on 28 Apr 1999 and bodies then **burned** and piled **into 15 foot high stacks**. Eye witness reports: Press report.*

17 Jun 1999: ***Daily Telegraph*** *features an interview with a Serb paramilitary 'soldier'. He and his 240 or so colleagues appear to be coarse* *and ill-educated drunks and drug abusers but well supported by Arkan. He shows little remorse for his actions which include murder, rape, and looting. His group are responsible for perhaps a 1,000 deaths. Eye witness accounts*

(18 June 1999) **The Express** *reports that 30 men were killed probably in May 1999, in the village of Zahac by Serb paramilitaries. They returned on 10 June 1999 and killed 4 women and 12 children (including a **1 year** old and **3 five year** olds (out of 12) and 2 more women also killed. Total deaths in the village appear to be 51. Extensive additional evidence of the killings (bloodstains etc). Eye witness account; Press report.*

19 June 1999; **The Express** *reports the experiences of Albanians held in the Lipjan prison. Extensive use of beatings (1 man stamped on his stomach until he died) and psychological torture (e.g. mock executions). Accommodation was badly over-crowded and unsanitary. Eye witness reports; Press report*

Lahuta* is an old single-stringed musical instrument.

VJ * Yougoslavian army

UQK * Kosovo Liberation Army (Ushtria Qlirimtare e Kosoves)

Shkau* singular, derogatory name for Serbian meaning ruthless

Shkie * Plural same as above

Qiftelia* is a two-stringed musical instrument